About

THE ONE THAT GOT AWAY

RHIANNE AILE • MADELEINE URBAN

THE ONE THAT GOT AWAY

Rhianne Aile • Madeleine Urban

Dreamspinner Press

Published by
Dreamspinner Press
4760 Preston Road
Suite 244-149
Frisco, TX 75034
http://www.dreamspinnerpress.com/

The One That Got Away

Cover Art by Paul Richmond   http://paulrichmondstudio.com

ISBN: 978-1-61581-085-7

Printed in the United States of America
Second Edition
November, 2009

eBook edition available
eBook ISBN: 978-1-61581-086-4

With greatest love
to both the families we were born to
and the families we have created.

A NOTE FROM THE AUTHORS

WHEN we first wrote *The One That Got Away*, it was for fun, meant to be posted on our brand-spanking-new blogs. Nothing angsty, nothing harsh. Just a light, enjoyable, sexy romance with the requisite happy ending.

We had no idea what we'd created.

It seemed like the people who read it on our blogs really liked it. When we looked at its publication potential, it didn't occur to us that people would miss it when it was gone. So when readers wrote us to ask about the story, it was sort of in limbo as we looked it over. We did think, briefly, about expanding the story at that time. It came in at about 52,000 words, a little short for a novel. But to us, the story was done. We'd written it from beginning to end and there it was, complete. Yes, call us naïve; we loved the story enough that we didn't want to mess with it. So we cleaned it up a bit and submitted it for consideration as an eBook.

Then it was published. And *holey moley*. Readers loved it.

Sure, we expected people would like it, but not so much! Our Inboxes were again full of mail, these glowing reviews started popping up, and we heard the inevitable question: why isn't *The One That Got Away* available in paperback?

And that leads us to now. This story was ridiculously popular, so popular that it surprises us to this day, and Dreamspinner offered us this incredible opportunity: a second edition. A chance to review the story, fix what we didn't like, polish what we did, and add another 15,000 or so words to flesh out the story of Trace and David's romance... and have it published in paperback.

We spent a lot of time trying to figure out what to do: Revise or rewrite? Polish or recast? Elaborate or plot? After several aborted starts, we decided to leave the bulk of the story intact. It's the story readers love, after all, and if we rewrote it, it wouldn't be *The One That Got Away* anymore.

So, if you read it in the first edition eBook, we hope you'll find this the same story you know and love—think of it as a director's cut with additional scenes. If this is the first time you've read *The One That Got Away*, we sincerely hope you enjoy it.

Lots of love, Rhianne & Madeleine

• Chapter 1

DAVID CARMICHAEL groaned when the bright sunlight hit his eyes as he walked from his office to *The Mirror*'s parking garage. His light blue eyes were sensitive anyway, and, today, when he needed them most, he'd left his sunglasses on the kitchen table. The fever and headache had started during the morning editorial meeting. By the time the news and features assignments were agreed on, he could barely focus. He hadn't suffered a migraine in almost a year, but he remembered the symptoms well. Telling his assistant he'd be out of the office for the rest of the day, he grabbed his keys and briefcase and headed home.

Pulling into his driveway, David folded himself out of his car, holding onto the door until the dizziness passed. He'd had to pull over twice on the way home to throw up and wanted nothing more than to pass out in a cool, dark room. Praying that he had some of his old prescription pills still in his medicine cabinet, he groped his way into the house and down the hall. He hadn't even bothered to bring his briefcase and cell phone inside. There was no way he was getting any work done today.

Ten minutes later, dressed in nothing but boxers, David ran a frustrated hand through his short blond hair, leaving it spiked up messily. Tearing open the bedside drawer, he plundered the contents, condoms and cigarettes and more falling to the floor. No medicine. "Fuck!" he swore. He could call the doctor and get some called in, but there was no way he could drive to the pharmacy.

Collapsing on the bed that was just too tempting to ignore, he reached for the phone. First he called his doctor's office. The nurse promised to call in a fresh set of refills for his prescription. Second, after a few moments' thought, he phoned Trace. If you couldn't call on your best friend to bring you medicine, when could you call him?

Trace was driving down Seaside Drive with the top down when his phone rang. He hit the button on his Bluetooth headset. "Trace Jackson," he said.

"Trace," David rasped. He rolled over so the phone was pressed between his ear and the pillow. He was too drained to hold it up. "I need your help."

"David? You sound like shit," Trace said, voice tinged with concern.

"Yeah." David shifted and swallowed down another wave of nausea. "I've got a migraine… bad."

"Hell. Been a long time since you had one of those. You got your meds? Where are you?" Trace asked.

"No, no meds. Can't find them, or I threw them out. It's been so long. The nurse called some in. Walgreens on Eighth." David paused to catch his breath. Even his own voice in his head was too loud.

"David, man, go lie down. Put a wet washcloth over your eyes or something. I'll pick up the meds. Anything else? Gatorade?" Trace asked as he pulled into a parking lot to turn around and head back to town.

"Already lying down, but the fuckin' bed is spinning. Just get me drugs."

"All right. I'll be there soon," Trace said, hitting the button to end the call and focus on traffic. He wanted to get there as soon as possible. It had been a long time since David had had a migraine, but when he got one, it was usually a doozy.

Half an hour later, Trace pulled his cobalt blue Mustang convertible up behind David's sporty sedan and hurried to the back door of the well-kept house, prescription bag in hand. Using his key, he went straight into the kitchen, tossed the bag on the counter, and filled a glass with cold water from the fridge dispenser. He tore open the bag and fumbled with the bottle, cussing the childproof top under his breath. Pills in hand, he grabbed the glass of water and headed back to David's room.

It was dim inside, the forest green drapes blocking out almost all the light, and Trace could see his friend curled up on the bed. "David?" he said softly, walking over to perch next to him on the edge of the mattress.

David moaned as the bed rocked. Cracking one eye open, he looked up at the tall, broad-shouldered man looking down at him, brows drawn together in worry. "I'm not dying," he croaked. "No matter how much I might wish it."

Trace winced. David's sunken eyes clearly reflected pain, and the laugh lines around those eyes and his mouth were heavily creased. "Here," Trace said quietly. "I bring pain relief."

"My hero." David reached for the pills, lifting up on his elbow to accept the glass and gulp down the water.

Nodding, Trace waited to take back the glass. After setting it on the nightstand, he ran his hand lightly over David's forehead. "You're hot too," Trace said. He stood up and went to the bathroom, wet a cloth with cool water, and brought it back to gently settle it over David's eyes.

David hissed as the cold cloth hit his overheated skin. His entire body shuddered. "Covers," he said, struggling to get up so he could get under the blanket.

Frowning, Trace took the cloth back and reached to pull down the sheets and quilted blanket while David slid his tense body under them. Trace pulled up the covers and tucked them around David's shoulders. "Sorry, man," he murmured. David looked really miserable.

"Thanks for playing errand boy. I'm sorry I interrupted your day. Go back to work. I'll live. I'm too ornery to die." David chuckled at his own joke and then winced as stabbing pain shot through his head until he was gasping. "Fuck," he panted, lying limp.

"I think I'll stick around, just in case. I've not seen you hurting this bad in a long time," Trace murmured as he resettled the cloth on David's forehead. "Humor me, okay?"

David would have glared at his friend if the muscles in his face didn't hurt so badly. Instead he settled for a small frown as a complaint and reached up to tug lightly on the tail of dark brown hair brushing over Trace's shoulder. "When was the last time you cut your hair, Jackson?" It was petty, but doing something as normal as picking on his friend's habit of wearing his hair so long it brushed below his shoulders made David feel just slightly better. It was a longtime tease; Trace didn't mind. He drifted to sleep with one corner of his mouth crooked up.

Trace's mouth quirked as David ribbed him. He held the cool cloth against David's face for a while and then set it aside. Sitting there, he decided he might as well work on his current project, so he went out to the car and got his laptop and notes. Once inside, he headed back to the bedroom to be close in case David needed him.

He kicked off his black dress shoes, shed his suit jacket, and pulled his tie loose, tossing it onto David's dresser. He snapped on the small shaded lamp on the nightstand and climbed onto the opposite side of the huge bed from David, booted up the laptop, slid his horn-rimmed glasses on, and settled in to work.

DAVID was kicked back in his upholstered office chair with his feet propped up on his desk, mostly asleep, and he could hear his assistant busily typing away on her keyboard. He decided he'd better get up before his back ached and started to move, but his feet were tangled in twisted-up phone cord. He started to fall....

Waking with a start that jarred his head as his eyes popped open, David cried out in pain as he attempted to sit up, his legs thrashing in the blanket wrapped around him.

As soon as David started moving, Trace dropped his pen and notebook and reached over, trying to calm him down. "David. Hey, you're okay," he said, trying to pull at the blanket so David wouldn't wrap it any tighter around himself. He held onto his laptop with his other hand, trying to keep it from sliding off his thighs.

Trace? What the fuck is Trace doing in my office? The two men had been friends for ages, but since they worked for rival newspapers, they never visited each other at work. "Trace? What? Why?"

"David," Trace said patiently. "C'mon. Wake up. You're hopped up on pain meds, man." He squeezed David's shoulder gently.

David blinked his eyes as the dimly lit room started swimming into focus. Trace was half-leaning over him. "Oh, wouldn't *The Mirror* just love to get a picture of this: *Warring newspaper correspondents found in bed together*. I can see the headlines now. Katherine would have her panties in a serious twist," David said, the words coming out sort of garbled. "Fuck, I'm thirsty. I feel like a circus train's traveled though my mouth." His head rolled to the side, landing against Trace's firm thigh instead of the thick, downy pillow usually there, and he yanked it back, causing a spike of pain and wave of dizziness.

"Careful," Trace cautioned, reaching out to help steady him. "You still look like hell. Hang on. I'll get you something to drink."

5

He set the laptop down on the bed and stood up gingerly, trying not to jostle the mattress. "Stay put," he ordered with a pointed finger before leaving the room.

"Like I have a choice," David muttered, sinking back against the pillows gingerly. Glancing at the alarm clock on the end of the dresser, across from the foot of the bed, he mentally calculated. He was at the supposed peak of the medicine's effectiveness, and the headache was still there—not as bad, but still there and strong. That didn't bode well. The prescription worked, but not for the full six hours before he could take another dose. And if two and a half hours in he still had symptoms this bad, it would be back with a vengeance in another two. He needed to try to eat while he might be able to keep food down, and it was probably foolish to try something that required a decent amount of balance, but he really wanted a shower too.

TRACE reentered the room carrying a tall glass of the decaffeinated iced tea David kept in the fridge. "Try this," he suggested, sitting on the edge of the bed near him. Sometime over the past couple of hours he'd pulled his hair loose of the band he used to tie it back, and he was wearing his glasses, something he hated doing around other people. But David had seen them before.

David smiled at him, that funny half-smirk. Trace knew it was another poke at his disheveled appearance. He had a self-styled, swanky, fashion-plate reputation that he wasn't living up to at the moment. It was one of the things that made their friendship so genuine—Trace was willing to look sloppy around David.

Reaching for the glass, David swallowed half of it in one gulp before his stomach lurched in protest. He set it carefully on the nightstand. "Thanks."

Nodding, Trace leaned on one hand on the mattress. "Pills not helping, huh?" Trace followed his eyes as David glanced at his reflection in the mirror across from the bed. Normally blond and hale and healthy, David's face had a gray tinge, and his eyes looked clouded. It was a big change.

David let his eyes close. "Oh, they're helping, but when I get one this bad, they just cut the pain. They don't kill it."

"Anything else help?" Trace asked, glancing at the floor as his sock-clad foot slipped on something. He pushed his glasses up absently, seeing the mess scattered around the nightstand. "I see you rifled the drawers looking for your pills," he said, reaching down to pick up the magazine his foot had touched.

"Would I ever hear the end of it if I asked you to rub my shoulders and maybe my scalp?"

Looking back to David before he turned over the magazine to see the front cover, Trace frowned slightly. "You're hurting, David. If I can help, it's no problem."

David rolled over and pushed the pillow out of the way so he could lie flat on the bed. "Thanks, Trace. At this point I'd even take the razzing. I owe you one."

Trace dropped the *American Journalism Review* in the drawer and paused long enough to scoop up the rest of the mess as well, raising a brow a bit at some of the dumped contents: pens and notebooks, of course; condoms and lubricant—he wasn't surprised at that; a half-empty bag of wintergreen candies; a lighter and a crumpled pack of cigarettes. Trace frowned. He thought David had quit. He dumped it all in the drawer before noticing something half under the bed, so he bent over a little more to reach for it.

Trace's fingers closed around something cool that felt like soft rubber, but it was cylindrical and…. He blinked when he pulled a dildo out from under the bed. His eyes flickered to David in surprise, but the other man was lying there with his eyes closed. Trace was tempted—really, *really* tempted—to start that expected razzing right now. He looked back down at it, heavy and thick and

7

about eight inches long, and then he laid it in the drawer and pushed the drawer closed.

Turning a little more to pull one knee up on the bed, Trace slid his fingers into David's hair and started rubbing gently with one hand before adding the other for a soothing massage. Meanwhile, he thought about what he'd found. There were easy answers, sure. There were also more… *interesting*… answers, knowing what he did about David. So, no. Probably not something to tease about. At least not right now. Trace kept his out-of-place musings silently to himself and smiled, amused by the direction of his thoughts.

David moaned, making a sound of sublime pleasure instead of pain for the first time since this headache had hit. "God, that's good. Just a little harder."

Now that his mind was on things erotic, Trace couldn't help but interpret the tone of David's voice in that context. As he strengthened the rubbing, he stifled a chuckle. He figured David had a healthy sex life, but it was just one of those things they hadn't happened to talk about over the years, especially since their tastes didn't mesh. Trace's social life was constantly the subject of gossip around town, so it was no surprise that David would be familiar with his friend's bed-hopping. Trace supposed he'd assumed that David was just private about his affairs. Nothing wrong with that.

The noises coming from the other man sounded pretty good to Trace—not that he'd ever heard another man during sex, with the exception of in a movie. He kept sliding his fingers over David's skull with one hand shifting through the gold-shaded hair, sliding the other down to the base of David's neck and lightly kneading with strong fingers.

David's shoulders rose into the touch, and he purred. Between the medicine and the light touch, he felt better than he had in hours. "You have fuckin' brilliant hands."

"So I've been told," Trace drawled, working more on David's neck.

David took a deep breath, relaxing into the physical attentions and the silence wrapped around him. As the massage relieved more and more of the pain, his body began reacting in a different way, his cock twitching where it lay trapped between his body and the mattress. David tensed, the pain returning slightly and dissuading his cock from its interest—which he knew was for the best. A good friend was a rare find, and Trace was the best. He and Trace had been friends for years without the slightest hint of sexual attraction. They were buddies, and David was absolutely certain Trace was totally straight. They talked politics and sports, not sex, and his friend had quite the social reputation that spoke for itself. Either way, David had no interest in losing his best friend over a quick roll in the proverbial hay. "I think maybe I'll try to take a shower while I still feel halfway decent," he mumbled into the sheet.

Trace's hands paused in their rubbing. "What do you mean, 'still'?" he asked, brow furrowing. "Is the migraine going to get worse?" he asked in concern, restarting the massage gently. It bothered him to see his best friend hurting so much.

"Yeah, if I can head them off in the first hour, sometimes one dose will make them go away, but when it gets a good foothold like it did today, it's usually more like twenty-four hours. The problem is that I can only take a dose every six hours, and the pain relief lasts four at best." David told himself he should move, but Trace's fingers felt so good that he couldn't bring himself to tell him to stop.

"What kind of for-shit meds are those?" Trace asked, exasperated. "All right. Get a shower. Sure I can't fix you something to eat?" He slowly eased his hands out of his friend's hair, not wanting to pull it accidentally and cause David any more pain.

"Yeah, I should try to eat. Check the pantry and see if I have any soup. Needs to be broth, not cream." David grimaced as he moved off the bed. "I'm gonna leave the door open. Between the headache and the meds, I might be a little unstable."

"Just be careful, David. You don't need a broken arm or something," Trace said, standing up and watching David cautiously to make sure he at least made it to the next room.

Once inside the soothing pale green and sandstone bathroom, David stripped out of his boxers and sat on the edge of the tub to keep from leaning over while he started the shower. He stood and stepped into the warm spray, braced his hands on the cool stone wall, and let the water sluice over his body. Between the medicine, Trace's hands, and the shower, he was actually feeling almost normal.

When he started to feel a little shaky, David finally shut off the water, got out of the tub, and reached for a towel to blot the skin of his upper body. Even the lightest pull on the curly blond hair blanketing his chest and belly hurt. It was amazing how sensitive a migraine made everything.

Bending down to dry his legs, the room started to spin. "Fuck," was all he got out as the world tilted and went black.

Trace was in the kitchen stirring the soup when he heard a loud thump. His eyes widened, and he dropped the spoon and ran, yanking himself around the corner and barreling down the hall into the bedroom and to the bathroom door. "Shit!" he swore when he saw David awkwardly sprawled on the floor. He knelt down and pulled David into more of a sitting position, feeling around the back of his head, relieved to find no blood.

Heart still pounding from the scare, Trace cursed under his breath and held David against his chest. "David. David?" He lightly patted the other man's cheek, unsure what to do other than call 911.

"Trace?" David mumbled.

Pinpoints of light, like the sparklers kids use on the Fourth of July, played on the dark backdrop of David's eyelids. His head was throbbing again and so was his shoulder. He could hear Trace's voice, but it sounded far away. "Trace?"

"David? Come on, open your eyes. Please? You're scaring the hell outta me."

David spoke, and his voice was gravelly. "I'm okay. Head just hurts like hell. The last thing I remember was being in the shower."

"Yeah, well, now you're on the floor. Did you hurt anything? Did you hit your head?" Trace looked over David's face anxiously.

"I don't know." David opened his eyes and winced, immediately closing them again. "My shoulder hurts too."

The quick flutter of David's eyes wasn't enough for Trace to judge his condition one way or another. "Which shoulder? The one you were lying on?" Trace slid his arm up to David's right shoulder, squeezing the joint gently.

"Ow! Fuck, yeah, that'd be the one. Flip the lights off, will ya, so I can hobble my way back to bed."

"I'm helping you this time. Shit, David. You could have broken something, or worse." Trace's voice was ragged with concern as he half-lifted David from the floor and helped him stay on his feet. Being a couple inches taller than David's six feet helped. It wasn't until he slid his arm around David's waist and his fingers settled on a bare hip that he realized David was still nude. *Well, it won't matter once he's between the sheets.*

Grateful for the support, David leaned into Trace's strength, the friction of his friend's clothes highlighting his own lack of covering. "Fuck," he muttered, whispering a silent prayer that their friendship would survive this day.

"What?" Trace asked, voice sharp with worry as they limped their way across deep green carpeting to the bed. "You okay? Something else hurting?"

"No, I just realized I was naked as a jaybird. You should be getting hazard pay for this visit." Sitting on the side of the bed, David nodded gingerly toward the dresser. "You want to get me some boxers so I don't offend your delicate sensibilities?"

Trace snorted. "Now I know you're drugged out of your skull. Me? Delicate sensibilities? I've got a set of the same gear myself. I think I'll survive the embarrassment." He reached up and pulled the sheets out of the way, waiting for David to shift and get under the covers. Then he grabbed three of the four pillows and propped David up on them.

Mostly satisfied that David was safely settled, Trace said, "I'll get the soup, if it's not scorched by now. I sort of dropped the spoon and ran."

"Okay," David said faintly as Trace left the bedroom.

The soup was indeed ruined, so Trace dumped it into the sink and started a new pot. It only took about ten minutes, and he headed back to the bedroom with two mugs and a sleeve of crackers. "Here you go. First-class service," he said drolly, setting the mug on the nightstand nearest David. Florence Nightingale was not a role he'd ever have cast himself in, but he figured he was doing an okay job. *Besides the whole letting him splat onto the bathroom floor thing.*

He walked around the bed and sat on the other side, carefully opened the crackers, and set the sleeve on the sheets between them.

"I can't believe your lovers let you get away with eating crackers in bed," David exclaimed, blowing the steam off the top of his soup.

Trace shrugged, munching on a crisp, salty wafer. "It's usually my bed, so I do what I want, right?" He sipped at the soup carefully before picking up a cracker and handing it to David. "Besides. You're not my lover, so all bets are off. No point in trying to impress you with my manners if I'm not going to score." He had a flash of sitting naked in bed with David for a reason other than illness, the easy camaraderie they shared spilling over into a more intimate relationship. Trace almost snorted his soup over the image and had to quietly laugh at himself.

David felt a momentary pang but dismissed it as a side effect of the migraine. His initial flippant retort died on his tongue. "No....

12

No, I'm not your lover, and based on your usual type that's not likely to change," he answered, his voice a little breathy.

Glancing sideways at David, Trace helped himself to another cracker. "So. Three hours until you can take another pill. You ought to try to sleep. I'll wake you up when it's time," he suggested, thinking about the progress he could make on his performance arts center impact report in the meantime.

Setting the still more-than-half-full mug aside, David slid down in the bed and pulled the cool sheets up. "Yeah. I think I'll try to do that. Lover or not, don't get crumbs in my bed, Jackson."

Trace watched David get comfortable and then went back to his soup without comment. It wasn't long before David's breaths evened out. Setting aside his empty mug a few minutes later, Trace watched David for a bit, still worried about him. Then he pulled his laptop within reach and got back to work.

The next thing he knew, a soft beeping woke him up slowly. He frowned, trying to figure out what it was and why he was so uncomfortable. He loved his soft, cushy, Sleep Number bed. Trace pried open his eyes. His focus was off because his glasses were skewed half off his face. He straightened them and looked around.

"Oh. Yeah," he murmured. He was at David's—in David's bed, actually—slumped against the smooth, polished headboard fully dressed and now totally wrinkled. The lamp on the table next to him threw soft light over the room, and the beeping was coming from his laptop's low battery alert. It was tilted onto its side, having slid off Trace's legs. Settling it in a more stable position, he looked down at his patient.

David lay curled up next to him, and his blond head was pillowed on Trace's thigh. Trace's arm was curled around him, his palm flat against David's back, practically holding him in place.

Trace was somewhat surprised by how David's head in his lap made his body take interest, but he dismissed it. He'd always been a really tactile person, and he carried on an active sex life. It was a great outlet for stress, and he enjoyed it. He'd made peace with his touchy-feely tendencies a long time ago.

Bemused, he drew a deep breath, trying to wake up, and yawned largely. A glance at the laptop's clock showed it was early evening. He must have dropped off while working on the report. Slightly annoyed by the beeping, he saved the open document, shut the laptop down, and carefully lifted it to set it on the nightstand but couldn't quite reach it without disturbing the bed. So he set it down next to him instead and turned his attention back to David.

David looked more relaxed, and some of the usual warm color was back in his face. Most of the pained creases were relieved, leaving just the trace of lines at the corners of his eyes and mouth from all his smiling. David's usually rugged features were softened in sleep, and without thinking about it, Trace rubbed David's back gently. He yawned again and thought about going back to sleep; he decided there was no reason not to and let himself doze off again after scooting down a little, dimly thinking about how warm David was against him.

• Chapter 2

DAVID woke into that warm, fuzzy, half-asleep place and contemplated letting the meds pull him back down. He remembered waking several hours earlier when the pain returned; Trace had brought him another pill and supported him while he drank enough water to get it down. Thankfully, the second dose had knocked him back out quickly. Taking a brief inventory of his body, he discovered that his shoulder hurt more than his head. He shifted into a comfortable position to get the pressure off it and—

Suddenly alert, David rubbed his cheek against smooth fabric, over something firm that was not his pillow. He opened his eyes cautiously. *Shit. Trace's leg.* He was trying to figure out how to gracefully extricate himself from his best friend's lap when he saw Trace staring down at him.

"Hey," Trace greeted him softly. "How are you feeling?"

"Ah, hey," David answered, his voice dry and raspy, one of the side effects of the medicine. "Seems like on top of everything else I've used you as a pillow." He pushed himself up slowly.

Trace smiled. "It's okay," he said, not moving out of place. "You look like you feel better."

"I do. I think I might even be hungry," David admitted with a smile. "I'm sure as hell sick of being in this bed. If I can make it to the kitchen table, think you could heat up some more soup?"

"Sure, just no unsupervised bathroom trips," Trace agreed good-naturedly. He needed to plug his laptop in anyway. He could duck out to the car and get the power cord. "Any other requests, your majesty?" he poked as he slid off the bed to stand, reaching above his head to stretch.

David turned with a cocky retort that evaporated as he watched Trace. His friend's lanky frame seemed to go on forever, extended like that, wide shoulders tapering down to narrow hips. His pale grey dress shirt had come untucked and the bottom two buttons pulled loose, revealing a triangle of tan skin bisected by a strip of dark hair. David swallowed. His mouth was dry now for a completely different reason.

Trace yawned as he stretched and tilted his head side to side, groaning when his neck popped audibly. He dropped his arms and rubbed the back of his neck with one hand. "Sleeping sitting up sucks," he muttered before stepping on a sock's toe with one foot to pull his foot free and then working off the other sock. He picked up his laptop and padded out of the bedroom barefoot.

Mute, David watched him leave. He needed to get Trace out of here. He couldn't imagine getting through the past eight hours without him, but the unusually close proximity for so long was obviously messing with his head. Swinging his legs over the side of the bed with a wince as he jarred his shoulder, he let the pain settle down to a dull ache before carefully donning a pair of boxers one leg at a time. His legs were still shaky as he followed after Trace.

Trace washed out the pot first and set it back on the stove before stooping over and spinning the lazy Susan, looking for another can of soup or two. More chicken noodle. Tomato. Cheddar broccoli. Chunky vegetable beef. *Yum.* He pulled out the can and leaned over a little more to see the selection on the bottom shelf.

David stepped into the kitchen, which was painted a deep wine red and trimmed with white crown molding, the work area surrounded by white cabinets that wrapped around three walls. He felt accomplished for making it that far. "Trace." His words stuttered to a halt.

Trace has an absolutely amazing ass. Bent over, one foot slightly raised for balance, his shirt was sliding up the broad, muscular back as he rummaged in the lazy Susan below the countertop. David would have to be a heterosexual saint to resist that image, and he was neither. His groin tightened, and he felt his cock go hard. *Fuck.*

"Hmmm?" Trace answered before standing back up with another can of soup, reaching to tuck his hair behind one ear. "You want vegetable beef or golden mushroom?" he asked, spinning the lazy Susan closed.

David swallowed the lump in his throat, unsure if it was the thought of food or the abrupt recognition of Trace's appealing appearance that had put it there. Trace's hand drew David's attention to the long, dark hair that he enjoyed ribbing his friend about. For the first time, he wondered how it would feel. Was it soft or coarse? He didn't remember from the times he'd yanked on it while teasing.

Sliding into a chair at the small kitchen table under the window, David let the table hide everything from his chest down. "Eww.... Yuck. I don't do mushrooms. That can has been in there since my mother came to visit three years ago. She uses it to make gravy. Vegetable beef, please." Trace nodded and turned to the pan, and David ended up looking at his rear again.

David sighed. *Thinking about Trace's ass is not a good idea.* He tried to think of something to talk about to remind himself that Trace was *not* gay. "So. What happened with Annemarie a couple weekends ago? Is she still around?" David asked.

Trace turned around to look at David. "It wasn't serious," he said. "She didn't... I mean, *I* didn't stick around. I don't do sticky," he said with an unrepentant smile.

David chuckled. "A different girl every week. Playboy," he teased.

Trace shrugged. "Nothing wrong with that. I never promise them anything more."

David tried to think of the last time he'd had sex and was having trouble remembering. "I think I'm getting old. The whole meeting and getting to know someone thing is just too much effort, and I'm not much of a casual-sex person."

Trace tapped the spoon on the edge of the pot and dropped it with a soft clink inside the empty soup can before turning around, giving David an incredulous look. "Old? David, you're what? Forty-two? Forty-three? That's nowhere near even approaching old. And there's nothing wrong with casual sex," he added, crossing his arms and leaning back against the counter. "As long as both people know up front, anyway."

"I'm not against it, and I agree with you, but... well...." How did you tell your best friend that you were, frankly, scared to death of AIDS? In pre-AIDS days, David had been what some would call promiscuous, but after watching more than one friend waste away and die, he couldn't bring himself to take the risk. He was clean, but it was purely luck. In the past decade, he hadn't been a monk, but he used condoms religiously and found himself wanting to know more and more about his lovers before he'd sleep with them. He stared at Trace. What could he say?

Raising a brow when David trailed off, Trace just tilted his head and turned back to the soup.

David's brow scrunched as he studied Trace's back. He was pretty sure Trace knew he was gay—they'd met up at town events from time to time with their respective dates—but sex wasn't a topic they talked about. Now David idly wondered why. Gay or straight, that was something guys usually went on about, comparing experiences and lovers and what they liked and didn't, wasn't it? That was how it was when David went out with his circle of friends; he supposed he assumed it was the same when Trace went out with his other friends. But it wasn't like that between the two of them. He mused about that while he watched Trace stir the soup slowly. David felt the hollowness of the silence that hung between them. It felt different. Before now they just hadn't spoken specifically about it. Now he felt like he was hiding something from his best friend.

"I'm gay," David blurted before he could think twice and back out of it. "I've seen too many friends become pale reflections of the men they once were because of AIDS. I guess it just makes me overly cautious." Keeping his eyes on Trace's back, he braced himself for the reaction.

Trace's hand stilled the spoon for a moment before restarting its movement. David could imagine what Trace was thinking. *Gay? David?* They'd known each other better than five years now. Now David kind of wished it had come up at some point, just to ease this awkward moment, just so he knew for sure that Trace knew.

Holding his breath, David bit his tongue. He didn't have to defend his life to anyone. If Trace couldn't deal with him the way he was, he'd be sad and probably pissed, but it wouldn't be the first time that someone had judged him.

Trace was watching the pot, and he tipped his head to one side before he answered. That had been quite a statement, coming from David, and Trace was glad the man trusted their friendship enough to share it. "Makes you smart, in my opinion," he said thoughtfully. "Can't be too careful these days."

David released his breath with a sigh. "Thanks," he said softly as he leaned back in his chair. They were going to be okay. *Thank God.* He should have known, really.

Trace let the spoon sit against the side of the pot as he picked it up. He grabbed two bowls off the open shelf where David kept his olive green stoneware dishes with his other hand as he turned to the table. "You're welcome," he said quietly as he poured out the soup.

Eating in silence, David felt something he hadn't felt in a really long time: completely comfortable.

Once he'd finished with his bowl, Trace got up and took it and the pot to the sink, washing them both out. Remembering the mugs in the bedroom, he headed back there to fetch them and clean it all up at once.

David watched him walk out of the kitchen and disappear into the hall. He sighed and got up to help with the dishes. He felt weak and drained, but not the least bit dizzy. Running some water into the pot in the sink, he went to move it to the other sink basin to soak while he rinsed the bowls. "Ow! Fuck!" he swore, stabs of sharp pain radiating from his shoulder and his arm going numb. The pot fell back into the sink with a heavy clunk and splash of water, and David leaned heavily against the counter for support.

Shocked by the loud, sudden noise, Trace hurried around the corner, a mug in each hand. "David? What's wrong?" He shoved the mugs he'd retrieved from the bedroom onto the counter, not even noticing the cold chicken noodle slopping over as he raised his hands to help.

Head hanging forward, his eyes tightly closed, David took several deep breaths. "Fuck, that hurt!" he swore, making his way over to the kitchen chair with Trace hovering, apparently worried about where he could safely touch the blond to help without hurting him. "I went to pick up the pot full of water and my shoulder.... Shit, I'm afraid I may have really screwed something up when I fell. When it's just at my side, it aches, but that was a sharp, stabbing, bring-tears-to-your-eyes-and-steal-your-breath kind of pain."

"Damn it, I was afraid something like this would happen when you insisted on that damn shower. C'mon. We're getting you dressed, and I'm taking you to the emergency room," Trace insisted, urging David toward the bedroom. "You might have broken something."

David stood there with his hurting arm cradled in the palm of his good hand. "You know, with the way this day is going, I'm afraid to get in a car. We'll never make it to the hospital in one piece." He chuckled mirthlessly; he was only half-kidding. With a weary sigh, he shuffled miserably to the bedroom. Picking out a worn pair of jeans, a T-shirt, and tennis shoes was no problem, but actually getting into them was proving to be a feat of painful mechanical engineering. Giving up, he swallowed his pride and called for Trace.

"I should've thought of that. Sorry," Trace murmured as he walked into the bedroom. He took the jeans from David and knelt down, pooling the legs so David could step into them, and he pulled the denim up over David's thighs to settle the waistband, even zipping and buttoning him up carefully before reaching for the T-shirt.

Biting his lip almost hard enough to draw blood, David tried to control his body's reaction to Trace's innocent touches. Every place where Trace's fingers brushed, his skin prickled with awareness. When the back of his hand grazed a nipple while maneuvering the T-shirt on without hurting his shoulder, David gasped, barely restraining a moan.

Trace grimaced. "Sorry, David," he murmured, figuring he'd pulled too hard. "You got any Birks or something to wear besides running shoes?" he asked, walking over to the closet, peering down at the floor, and then bending over to sort through the jumbled shoes.

David really wished that Trace would quit presenting him with images of his ass, dress pants stretched tightly over very firm muscle. His eyes closed on a sigh. "Yeah, there's a pair in the back corner."

David rested a hand on Trace's shoulder for balance while slipping his feet into the sandals. "Let's get this over with."

"SIX hours. Six fucking hours. Good thing what was wrong with me wasn't life threatening," David complained, sliding out of Trace's car, which was finally back in David's driveway.

Trace just humored him with a "Mmm-hmmm," not even rolling his eyes. When he'd broken his arm a few years back, he'd sat in the ER for twice that long before seeing anyone. "I'll get that," he said, plucking the pharmacy bag out of the car before David could lean over to get it. "No more bending over for you."

"And exactly how are you planning on pulling that one off?" David teased, leaning against the side of the car. His right arm and shoulder were wrapped up to hold them still and close to his body. As Trace locked the doors, David added, "Living tends to involve at least a little bending over." David giggled at the double meaning of the words, punchy from the pain meds they'd given him at the hospital.

Grinning, Trace walked around the front of the car, shaking his head a little. "You're looped, man. Come on. Inside with you. You're on bed rest for a few days." He took David by the good arm and made sure he got up the steps and through the back door. Trace nudged him through the kitchen, past the dining room with its large, round marble-top table, through the corner of the comfortable living room, and down the hall toward his bedroom.

"Well, I must say it's refreshing to have a man trying to get me to bed who *doesn't* want me to bend over." David chuckled, kicking off his Birks and stretching out on the bed with a sigh. "Ahhh.... Tired...."

Trace smiled and pushed David's legs under the sheets, pulling the covers up over him. "Just try not to roll over on that shoulder, huh? I don't want to be awakened by a howling shriek," he joked.

David mumbled something unintelligible and was asleep before Trace left the room. With a small smile, Trace pulled the door shut and went to the kitchen to make a note to himself to call David's boss tomorrow, telling him what happened. He'd ask his own boss about working half-days next week; Trace had plenty of comp time to claim. He'd go in tomorrow—actually today, since it was three a.m.—to finish up his big project piece for Sunday.

Exhausted, Trace figured he could catch a few hours' sleep, so he turned off the lights, unbuttoned and unzipped his pants to be more comfortable, and lay down on the couch to sleep.

The second time he caught himself almost sliding off the overstuffed leather, he got up with a muffled curse and walked back to the bedroom. He had to get some sleep or he'd have crap for brains. He pushed the door open to look in at David. He had that huge bed to himself. There was plenty of room for them both. Hell, Trace could practically lay out spread-eagle and still not touch David, it was so wide. "What the hell's he need a bed this big for, anyway?" he muttered as he walked into the bedroom.

He pulled his shirt and pants off before crawling under the sheets in his black low-ride briefs and white undershirt. As he settled down to sleep, it occurred to him to wonder how many other men had slept in this bed. But the thought slipped away before he could form any sort of opinion on it.

DAVID attempted to roll onto his back, and a twinge from his injured shoulder woke him fully. He groaned in pain and swore under his breath. The doctor had said at least six weeks to heal, maybe eight to nine, with at least a full week of bed rest starting now. *Fuck.* How was he going to get by? Shifting to move the weight cutting off circulation to his leg, he backed into something solid and warm. Glancing over his wrapped right shoulder, he blinked bleary eyes, seeing mussed, dark hair. For a long moment, he was totally disoriented. Oh. Right. Trace, on his back, sound asleep. Apparently they'd slid together as they slept, and Trace had rolled over right up against David's back. *Well, at least it kept me off this shoulder.*

David told himself to pull away, but leaning back against the sleep-heavy weight was very comforting. Closing his eyes, he drifted back to sleep.

The first thing David noticed upon waking the next time was Trace's absence. He'd woken several times during the night, Trace's warm presence helping him fall back to sleep. As he pushed himself into a sitting position, he could hear Trace talking in the other room but couldn't make out the words. Swinging his feet to the floor, David stood up slowly, his left hand gripping the curved footboard for balance. Once he was steady, he headed toward the smell of coffee and Trace's deliberately hushed voice.

"… yeah, six to eight weeks, maybe more. The doctor's office said they'd fax over the paperwork for the short-term disability. Sure. Yeah, he's got… a friend to stay over. Help him around the house and all. Yeah, I'll tell him. Sure thing." Trace closed his phone with a snap and looked up from where he sat at the kitchen table, dressed in his trousers and undershirt, to see David standing in the doorway. "Hey, handsome. How you feeling?" he asked with a warm smile.

Momentarily stunned by the smile and the endearment, it took a moment for all of Trace's conversation to sink in. Not wanting to assume that Trace was talking about himself, David asked a more mundane question. "Were you just talking to Lloyd?"

"Yes. He said to stay still and get better, though you can still review editorials and write your column if you're up to it. But if he sees you in the office before the eight weeks are up, he'll do something nasty and unprintable with your corpse," Trace said with a grin. "Sit down, David. You're not even supposed to be out of bed."

David shivered at the idea of Lloyd doing anything "unprintable." "Dirty old coot! It's just my shoulder. If I have to stay in bed for two months, I'll be certifiable."

"You're supposed to be in bed for *one week* to keep your shoulder stabilized. That's why you're wrapped up like a Thanksgiving turkey, ya goof. Sit down." Trace stood and went to pour David a cup of gourmet coffee, mixing it with cream and sugar, the way he knew the other man liked. Turning back to the table, he surveyed David's pale face. "You want something to eat? You should have something in your stomach before you take more painkillers."

"Wonder what I could get for them on the street?" David mused as he slid carefully into a chair. "I could use a new laptop." Trace laughed. Chuckling, David reached for the mug with his good hand, staring down at the pale tan liquid. Taking a tentative sip, he hummed his approval. Trace knew the way David liked his coffee.

When Trace opened the refrigerator and started pulling out sandwich fixings, David remembered that he was due to go to the grocery store, or he'd be living on unhealthy delivery food and hearing no end of it from Trace. He glanced up at his friend and watched Trace pull a jar of white stuff out of the fridge and frown at the blue and red label.

"David, why do you have Miracle Whip in your fridge when you don't like anything but real mayonnaise?" Trace asked as he set jars of condiments and packages of cheese out on the counter. "And tomatoes? Didn't you tell me you don't like tomatoes on your hamburgers? Or was it tomato sauce?" His brow furrowed as he set the deli-sliced meat on the island with a loaf of nine-grain bread.

Trace's questions left David blank until he remembered a reception they had both attended at the Williston Hills Country Club after the regional polo tournament, Trace working the social gathering, David representing the editorial board of his newspaper. Snatching a small patch of shade under a giant oak tree, David had complained to Trace about the chicken salad being made with Miracle Whip—a crime for a caterer, but most likely a nod to the overly hot weather—and apparently Trace remembered.

"Don't you ever forget anything, Jackson?" David said, shaking his head. "The mayonnaise is in the door. The Miracle Whip was for—aw, hell—some guy I was seeing for a while. I should've known he was a jerk when he said he'd only eat Miracle Whip. And I like tomatoes, just not on sandwiches. I slice 'em up on a plate with salt, pepper, and vinegar."

Trace shrugged, grabbed the jar of Miracle Whip, and nonchalantly tossed it in the trash before he nabbed the mayo and a tomato. David laughed as the jar went sailing.

"Just stuck with me, I guess," Trace said. "You don't complain about things, so I remembered," he said, distracted as he pulled a knife from the block and started slicing the tomato on the butcher block.

David grinned. "Thanks. I should've had you over the night I threw him out too. You make it look so easy."

Both Trace's brows rose as he started building sandwiches. "That doesn't sound too good, having to throw him out," he observed. "But I would've helped."

"Yeah, I think you would've. I kind of like having a built-in valet, cook, and chauffeur. Think I could afford you?"

"I don't know...." Trace drew out the words doubtfully. "Takes a lot to keep up my high-class lifestyle," he said, winking as he pulled a few plates down from the shelf. David snickered. Trace lived in a two-room studio apartment. A fancy one in a nice high-rise, but not what David would consider "high-class."

"So, what's for lunch?" David asked, reaching for the flatware and napkins in the caddy on the table and setting two places one-handed.

"Turkey and Swiss," Trace said, pulling a bottle of vinegar out of the cabinet. He walked over and set it on the table along with the plate of sliced tomatoes and moved the salt and pepper shakers within David's reach. "Drink?" he asked as he headed to the fridge.

It struck David, all of a sudden, how comfortable this was. Of course, they'd hung out on free Saturdays quite a few times, grilling steaks or burgers on David's backyard deck and talking and watching movies or something, so he supposed it wasn't any big change.

David belatedly remembered Trace's question. "What I really want is a beer, but that's probably not a good idea with the pain meds. Pepsi." Surprisingly hungry, David started eating, and three-quarters of his sandwich was gone before he realized it. He looked at Trace while reaching for the tomatoes, now that he had room on his plate. "So when do you need to leave? That hard-ass boss of yours probably sees this as fraternizing with the enemy." George Hardin, the executive editor of Trace's newspaper, *The Sun-Herald*, was Trace's boss and was widely known as very staunchly supporting a cutthroat, competitive stance against David's paper, *The Mirror*, and by natural association, its executive editor, Lloyd Morton. Having him for a boss, David counted his blessings often that Lloyd was considerably more laid-back.

Trace glanced up from his sandwich, waiting to answer until he'd finished chewing. "No reason to tell him who I'm helping," he said with a shrug. "Unless you've got someone else to call, I'm sticking around."

"I do have a friend or two besides you, Jackson. I could probably set up a rotation of guys who could drop in and check on me," David mused, silently acknowledging that most of his friends really weren't the nurturing type. Although he *was* somewhat surprised at Trace's natural nursing ability... and inclination.

"Yeah, that sounds promising. You really need to be in bed, David," Trace said, concern marking his brow. "If you move that shoulder, even a little, and get it out of alignment, you might have to have surgery to put it back together. I think I'll stick around."

"I'll make you a deal," David bargained. "I'll get back in bed. I'll even let you give me one of the pain pills that will knock me out for a few hours. You can go check in with your editor before he puts out an APB and then pick us up a stack of movies and Huwan Cho's Chinese for dinner on the way back."

"Sounds good to me. Now finish your lunch." Trace grinned and poked the plate of tomatoes closer before sliding out of his chair to pry open one of the prescription bottles. That was an easy enough bribe to keep David in bed for several more hours. "You want sesame beef or pork lo mein?" he asked, knowing David's usual favorites. "I'll get some pot stickers and steamed vegetables too."

"How about both and we'll share them?" David suggested, well acquainted with Trace's habit of snagging food off his plate. Finishing up the last of his sandwich and the tomatoes, he took the pills with the end of his soda. Standing, he shuffled, obviously stalling. He wanted to ask something.

Trace rinsed the plates off in the sink and stacked them to wash later. When he turned, he saw David waiting. "Do you need something?" Trace asked in concern. David didn't look like he felt all that well, but he looked better than he had some hours ago. Trace tilted his head to one side, his hair tumbling off his shoulder and the wrinkled T-shirt he'd slept in.

"Could you…. That is, would you… erm." David fidgeted. "Can you help me get my jeans off?" he blurted out. The button fastening on the close-fitting jeans made using one hand almost impossible.

Smirking, Trace set his hands on his hips. "You know, I would have figured you for a more suave kind of guy," he teased. "What kind of line is that?" he asked as he walked over and handily unfastened the button. "I wouldn't figure guys would be so easy," he said as he pulled down the zipper.

David watched as Trace's long, blunt fingers unbuttoned his jeans. His breath lodged in his throat, making his head spin, and he could feel his cock, only fractions of an inch from Trace's fingers, start to swell. *Fuck.* Forcing air into his lungs, he glanced guiltily up at Trace's face. His friend was grinning at him, relaxed, teasing. Trace had no idea the effect he was having on him. *Thank you, God.* "Yeah, well, then you don't know men very well. We're an easy bunch when it comes to getting in our pants."

Trace laughed and slid two fingers through a belt loop on David's hip, tugging gently to get him moving toward the bedroom. "Well, I guess I should've known, since that includes me. But I'll keep it in mind should I ever decide to expand my horizons."

Something flip-flopped in David's gut. Trace teasing about becoming bi-curious was doing nothing to calm his libido. Hopefully the meds would kick in soon and knock him out.

After following Trace down the hall obediently, David pushed his jeans to the floor, walked out of them as he crossed the bedroom, and crawled immediately into bed. He didn't open his mouth for fear his muddled brain would say something he couldn't take back.

Straightening the sheet out from under the quilted blanket, Trace pulled it up over David. He sat on the edge of the bed, leaned over David to snag another pillow, and pushed it up carefully under David's injured shoulder. "There you go," he murmured, squishing the pillow a little more before looking at David. "Think you'll be okay? I've got to go out for awhile."

David felt Trace's warm body close and resisted the urge to scoot closer. "I'll be fine. Go. Before Hardin fires your sorry ass and you have to move in with me when you lose that high-class apartment."

Trace chuckled quietly. "All right. I'm going. I've got my cell." He reached over and turned out the lamp, walked over to the bathroom to turn on the light and pull the door partly closed, and then sighed softly. At least David would be okay. Seeing him hurt really bothered Trace. Mouth quirking fondly, he left David to sink into sleep.

• Chapter 3

IT TOOK five days of David's forced restriction for he and Trace to develop a routine. Trace left for a few hours in the morning and a few more in the afternoon to get his work done, making sure he was at the house to deliver a meal or do the cooking for lunch. In the evenings they were working their way through a tall stack of DVDs Trace had brought back that second night. Now, after about a week, Trace had almost gotten used to being around the house all the time. It was all so… domestic.

"The popcorn almost ready or should I hit pause?" David called out from the living room.

"Pause, please!" Trace said, loud enough for David to hear as he blankly watched the microwave tick down the time. His mind was on work tonight—in between occasional thoughts about David—and he doubted he'd actually comprehend the movie, although he'd sit and watch it to keep David company. David was trying hard not to be a bear, he could tell. It was kind of funny, really.

Blinking when the microwave beeped, he realized he was grinning. Shrugging, he pulled out the hot and steamy bag, tossing it from hand to hand until he got it open and into a large plastic bowl, one of several in David's cabinets.

It was *different* staying over at David's. They got along really well in close quarters, so far anyway, like they'd been sharing a house for much longer. Trace had decided he liked having the company, even if it was quiet, somewhat-unlike-David company. And it beat going home to an empty apartment. He was a social creature and had always thought David was the same, but now he realized he really didn't know that for sure. Yeah, they got along fine, but there wasn't a circle of friends around the two of them. Trace had his—and, in theory, David had his. Trace wondered what else David did besides hang out with him. He hadn't had much at all in the way of visitors, as far as he knew, just a few guys from the office David had mentioned visiting while Trace was at work. Definitely no one who would be considered a lover, Trace suspected, because a lover would have been here instead of him. Even if David wasn't into casual sex, surely he got in some companionship somehow.

Something more than Trace sleeping in his bed an arm's length away.

Trace walked over to the fridge for cold drinks, pulling it open. *Hmm. Grocery run needed.* He added it to his list of things to do tomorrow. He needed to go home and wash clothes and clean the litter box and feed the cat, who was really giving him hell over being gone so much. Mabel could be such a bitch sometimes. Or whatever the cat equivalent was. It seemed wrong somehow to call a cat a bitch. He needed to pick up his suits at the cleaners, conduct a series of interviews at the renovated art museum, turn in the latest set of music reviews, make a list of pending restaurant reviews, pick up some more DVDs....

With all this bouncing around in his head, he was distracted when he walked into the living room, carrying two drinks and the big bowl of popcorn, and he was taken completely by surprise when he ran into the coffee table. He flopped backward, popcorn and soda flying up into the air in slow-motion like a bad comedy routine as he thumped to the carpeted floor.

32

David watched in horror as Trace tripped. Without thinking, he reached out to help, cursing as pain knifed through his shoulder, his arm dropping limp to his side. "Fucking hell," he hissed, dropping back onto the couch.

Groaning, Trace rolled over onto his back and stared up at the ceiling. "Ouch," he mentioned conversationally.

"Yeah," David agreed, his voice a little shaky. "Who are we going to get to move in and take care of us if both of us get hurt?"

Trace turned his chin to look up at David. He sounded like he was hurting. He'd been fine five minutes ago. "You okay?" he asked, his face lined with concern.

"No, actually, it hurts like hell." David swallowed. "I sort of lurched to get up and help when you started falling." Damn, he was getting tired of always whining. Extending his good hand to Trace, he shifted forward to help him up and looked at the soft drinks. "I think we need something stronger, don't you?"

"Yeah, I think so too," Trace said, wincing when David helped haul his butt up. He looked down at the scattered popcorn and was thankful he hadn't opened the soda cans. "Let me get this cleaned up, and I'm going to the liquor store. You'll have to skip the Vicodin if you want to drink, though," he told David as he leaned over to pick up the bowl and scoop most of the popcorn off the carpet.

"I'll live, and you don't have to go to the liquor store. I've got a stocked cabinet under the CD player. My poker club doesn't do the cheap stuff." David pointed to a set of doors in the entertainment center. "Unless you really just need to get out for a bit, which I'd totally understand," he added.

Trace completely missed David's last comment as he finished scooping up popcorn and set the bowl aside. "Poker club?" he asked as he walked over to the CD player he'd used many times over the years. "I didn't know you played poker. Much less in a club." He crouched down and opened the cabinet. "Holy shit, David! What kind of poker is it, high stakes?" he asked in surprise. The lines of bottles inside weren't even of the not-cheap variety; they were of the damn-expensive variety. "Jesus," he muttered as he started shifting bottles around.

David shrugged the best he could with one shoulder. "It's a group of guys I grew up with. We play pretty high stakes, yeah, but over the years, I'd guess we're all pretty close to even. Jared's on a roll right now, but he needs it. His ex fleeced him last year."

Trace glanced over his shoulder, somehow both happy to know for sure that David had other friends, but a little jealous that he wasn't included. He held out a bottle. "What do you want? I've never even tried most of this stuff. Kentucky bourbon's about as good as it gets on my paycheck."

"Second one from the right with the black label," David instructed. "You should try it. Collecting rare and exclusive single malts has become sort of a hobby among the group. Whenever we travel, we bring something back. The rule is you bring a bottle for everyone in the group."

Trace's brows were up in his hairline. "A bottle for everyone in the group?" he exclaimed as he pulled out the requested bottle. "Dear God. You better hope you win that night." He stood up after grabbing a couple of glasses from another shelf. "Ice?" he asked.

"Ice!" David barked, outraged. "Sacrilege! If you want to water down your scotch, there's a bottle of Jack Daniels from the corner liquor store in there somewhere."

"Geez, okay, okay!" Trace answered, thumping the bottle down on the coffee table in front of David. "Give the uneducated a break. I didn't play cards and drink hard liquor in school. I was poor." He unscrewed the cap and handed it over to David. "Hell, I'm still poor. Must be why I'm an arts reporter. I hit all the swank parties on my expense account."

"How do you think we got un-poor?" David laughed. "Every one of us paid our way through college playing poker and pool."

34

Trace grinned as David filled the glasses. "Somehow I never would have taken you for a shark, David. Isn't that interesting?" he drawled, sitting on the couch next to him and propping his feet up on the table.

"We're playing in a couple weeks. If you're still around...." David's voice trailed off. He wondered if Trace would accept. He'd thought of asking him before but had never followed through with it. Now David wondered why.

Is that an invitation? "I figure I'll be here unless you're miraculously healed, but I'd be a third wheel. I don't know anything about poker except how to make a full house." Trace's brow furrowed. "Maybe."

When David grinned, Trace was immensely pleased that he'd just decided to be available. He'd always felt like David valued his privacy, and Trace had taken pains not to presume or invade too much. It made him feel better to know David still wanted him here.

"There's a deck of cards in the side table drawer. You'll have to shuffle, but I can teach you enough to get by," David offered. He was ridiculously happy that Trace had agreed to attend. Having him around was easy, enjoyable, even a little addictive.

Trace leaned over to dig into the drawer. "All right, but no laughing. I spent much more time flipping quarters and making out than playing cards," he warned. He moved to sit on the floor across the low coffee table and set the deck in between them, reached for his glass, and took a cautious sip. He immediately moaned and closed his eyes. "Aw, hell. I'm ruined for life."

David's mouth quirked. "Good scotch and a good lover will ruin you every time," he murmured, cutting the deck. His arm was still tingling from his earlier foolish move, but the pain had subsided to a low throb.

Trace grinned. He happened to agree, at least with the second part of the sentiment. "I'll shuffle and deal. Don't mess with that shoulder," he said, wiping his bottom lip with the back of his hand before taking up the cards.

"We'll start with five-card stud," David announced.

"I'm going out on a limb and guessing five cards each," Trace said drolly. "What are we going to bet with?"

"Popcorn?" David suggested, reaching for what had been salvaged back into the bowl and dumping even piles in front of them. Throwing three pieces in the center, he popped another five into his mouth. "Ante up. That's what you have to bet to play the hand."

Trace followed suit with three pieces and half a handful in his mouth. "Okay. Five-card stud. Heh." He tilted his head, eyes flashing in amusement, and decided to take advantage of the relaxed situation to prod for information. "This group of yours... do the guys all stand stud?"

Chuckling, David fanned his cards, examining them. "Ha, maybe once upon a time. Most are married—until last year, when Jared's wife left him, and he's still too torn up to even think about dating. Out to pasture might be a better description."

"Except you," Trace pointed out as he looked at his cards and moved a couple around, leaning his elbows on the table.

"Yeah, well.... You've seen the hordes lining up at the bedroom door. Why would I want to give that up?" David picked up four pieces of popcorn and tossed them in the center. "I'm in."

They paused when Trace belatedly remembered he'd need his glasses, and then David gave Trace a brief outline of the hierarchy of hands and how to bet. Trace was pretty sure he could remember it all, but he was definitely sure David would be happy to remind him... and tease him at the same time.

When they got back to the game, Trace said, "Now that I think about it, I've actually noticed, sometimes. When someone had your attention." He frowned at his cards but threw in some kernels anyway before taking a drink.

David tilted his head, looking at his friend speculatively. "You have?"

Trace looked up from his cards and shrugged a little. "Just some times when you were in a better mood than usual, I figured you'd found someone. When you passed on ball games on the weekend, that sort of thing. Then, I thought it was a woman." Trace grinned. "But same result."

"Hmmm. So I guess that means those mornings that you couldn't sink a putt to save your soul but grinned anyway came after marathon sex sessions," David speculated.

"Could be," Trace said, eyes bright. "I'd already hit a hole in one," he added smugly as he sat back with his glass.

David was sipping his scotch, and he choked after Trace's bad pun. "Oh, God, Jackson, that's bad even for you. I call."

About twenty minutes and several hands later, David scraped in the pot and raised another handful of the salty kernels to his mouth. "We seem to be running out of currency," he commented, peering at the nearly empty bowl.

Trace chuckled as he emptied his glass and looked down into the bowl. "Well, we could always play strip," he joked as he tossed another handful into his mouth, hair scattering over his shoulders.

Tipping his head back, David downed the rest of his scotch in one gulp, his pulse racing at the thought of Trace naked. *Fuck, why not?* he thought, deciding to call the cocky bastard's bluff. "Works for me. We'll skip the ante and just play hands. Whoever loses the hand loses a piece of clothing. That work for you?"

Shrugging, Trace reached for the bottle and tipped a bit more into each glass. "Go for it. You're the shark," he teased. He shuffled the cards, dealt, and looked at his hand after another drink. His cheeks were warm, like he'd had three or four good beers already. It felt good to just have fun again. He looked up at David with an honest smile as he waited.

Face schooled to go blank, David looked at his cards seriously for the first time that night. He hadn't been letting Trace win, but he hadn't been taking his usual risks either—the risks that usually paid off. Flicking the edges of his cards, he folded them face down on the table. "I'll take two."

Trace gave David two cards, and then he looked at his own. *Strip poker with David. What a crazy-ass thing to do when I barely know how to play the game.* He traded out one, chuckled, and shrugged. "I took one."

David flipped over his cards, trying not to smile. "Aces and nines."

Wrinkling his nose, Trace looked at his cards and shook his head. "Just eights." He looked down at his clothes and shrugged, pulling off a black dress sock and dropping it to the floor.

"Oh no," David chided. "Anything that comes in pairs, goes in pairs. Take 'em both off."

Trace rolled his eyes and yanked off the other sock, exposing long toes that sank into the thick carpet as he pulled up one knee to lean on. "Picky, are you? Fine. I'll remember that," he said after another sip of scotch. He shuffled and dealt.

Five hands later, David looked at Trace over the top of his cards, eyes narrowed. Trace had lost his socks, his dress shirt, his belt, and his watch. The next thing to go would be the thin white T-shirt that was stretched across his well-defined chest. David wasn't sure he could take it. As for himself, he'd started off with nothing but jeans and a T-shirt, and he'd already lost the T-shirt. "I call."

"All right," Trace said, setting down the glass he'd emptied of scotch again before he fanned out his cards. "Three of a kind," he crowed.

"Nice. Very nice," David agreed. Pressing his cards to the table with a flourish, he smirked. "Just not quite good enough. Flush of hearts."

Trace's face fell comically. "I thought I had you that time," he pouted, shaking his head so his hair flopped over his shoulders. He tossed down his cards and pulled the T-shirt out of his waistband and over his head, laying it over the arm of the couch as he reached for the cards to shuffle again.

David knew it just didn't occur to Trace to be uncomfortable. He wore shorts and tanks when he and David played racquetball. He'd even been in clinging, soaked swimming trunks when they'd gone to the water park. *Oh, wrong thought, Carmichael.*

David shifted uncomfortably on the couch and couldn't drag his eyes from Trace's smooth, tanned chest. It was obvious that he'd stepped up his workout routine; he hadn't been nearly this defined last summer. David shifted again, reaching for his glass of scotch and finding it empty. He either needed to get drunk really quickly or get out of this room. Not wanting to waste exquisite scotch, he opted for the latter. "I think maybe it's time for bed. The meds mixed with alcohol are getting to me," he stammered, standing.

Trace blinked owlishly through his glasses as he watched David get up. "Okay," he said, sounding a little concerned. "Are you all right?" he asked, seeing the other man's flushed face but easily attributing it to the scotch.

"Ah, yeah." David shook his head, still hesitating beside the couch. He needed help with his jeans unless he wanted to sleep in them, but Trace's hands anywhere near the vicinity of his crotch was just not a good idea right now. Making a silent vow to wear sweatpants the next day, he cleared his throat. "Um, if you'll just undo the button, I think I can handle the rest," he said, motioning toward his jeans. He was half-hard but hoped Trace just wouldn't notice. The man was straight, after all; he wasn't going to be looking for signs of arousal from a man.

"Sure." Trace pushed away the niggle of concern. He'd probably been mother-henning David too much anyway. If the man was tired, he was tired. He shifted to his knees, reached up, and slid his fingers into the waistband on both sides of the button as he pulled it open. It did occur to him to glance over what he was doing. Some part of his head noticed, "Hey, David's got some size on him," but as soon as he released the jeans and sat back, the thought was gone. "I'm gonna chill awhile, then I'll clean up." He smiled lazily. "Thanks for the scotch."

David swallowed, looking down at Trace. His eyes were closed, and his mouth was curved up into a satisfied smile. David was nearly overcome with a desire to lean down and kiss those plump lips. Clenching his fists, he forced himself to turn away from his friend and walk toward the bedroom, adjusting the growing tightness in his jeans once his back was turned. If his right arm had been functioning properly, he'd have locked himself in the bathroom and taken care of the developing problem, but annoyingly, he wasn't at all ambidextrous when it came to self-pleasure. Once safely hidden away in his bedroom, he shuffled his jeans to the floor, cursing softly as his hand brushed the bulge in his boxers, torturing himself by letting his fingers linger and flex over the stiff shaft. "Fuck. Fuck. Fuck." He stretched out on the bed.

Humming slightly as he enjoyed the buzz, Trace lay sprawled on the couch for some time before yawning and deciding he should move before he fell asleep right there. He stretched and yawned again, then knelt down on the floor, and cleaned up the rest of the popcorn, secreted away the scotch, and scooped up his clothes. Turning off the light, he wandered down the hall, stopping to drop his clothes in the hamper in the hall closet. With a sigh he pushed the bedroom door open and peered in at the figure under the covers. David had taken to sleeping on his good shoulder, uncomfortable on his back, and the soft light from the bathroom fell on his blond hair. Trace slid his hand into the bathroom and clicked off the light before walking around to the other side of the wide bed.

An audible shift of clothing told David that Trace was slipping out of his pants, leaving them puddled on the floor, and crawling into bed in just his briefs. Then Trace sighed and stretched out on his belly, pulling the pillow under his chin.

David shifted as the bed dipped under Trace's weight, keeping his breathing even so that Trace would think he was already asleep. He'd been lying in the dark trying to make sense of his conflicting thoughts. He and Trace had been friends for years without the hint of something more, and now, suddenly, he was assailed by erotic thoughts of stripping the handsome brunet bare and licking every inch of his body. Biting his lip, he moved his leg slightly forward to hide the evidence of his wayward thoughts. But he cracked open his eyelids when Trace sighed.

Trace curled his body toward David unconsciously, drawn by the heat of the other man's body. After a few long minutes, he shifted further in David's direction as he slept. Tensing as Trace threw an arm over him some minutes later, David bit back a moan. *Oh, great. Feed Trace decent scotch and the man becomes a cuddler.*

David attempted to inch sideways to put more space between them, but Trace's arm resting at his waist tightened and pulled him back into the curve of his body. With a resigned sigh, David attempted to relax. It felt good to be held, and he was asleep before he knew it.

• Chapter 4

IT WAS late the next morning before Trace stirred, shifting slightly against the warm body he held close. It didn't occur to him to be confused. He hummed slightly, nuzzling the neck in front of him before stilling again, drifting along in a light sleep. His dream was one of pleasant satiation and rest; Trace purred softly and pulled the warm body closer, pressing his lips gently to the side of the neck. He wasn't conscious enough to really be awake.

Sighing, Trace cuddled closer, inhaling deeply. It was warm and pleasant, having someone he really cared about so close, though he was too far asleep, even in his dream world, to open his eyes and look at his lover. His hand curled over the body's waist, flattened, and rubbed ever so slightly over warm skin.

The sudden shift of the bed and the body confused him, and it took him a long moment to figure out what was dream and what was real as he pushed himself to sit up and open his eyes. He blinked, seeing immediately that David was gone and that he was in the middle of the bed instead of on his side. A groggy glance told him the bathroom door was shut, so he turned over, scooted to the cooler sheets on the far side, and curled back up around the pillow. He hoped he could have that dream again. It was warm and comfortable and smelled familiar, a smell that he instinctively recognized as belonging to someone dear to him. But he drifted back off before his brain could connect the scent with a name. Trace sighed happily as he sank back into the dream, pleased by the arms that curled around him, the scent filling him and making him feel like he was where he was supposed to be.

CALMING the pounding in the lower part of his body with several deep controlled breaths, David leaned back against the bathroom door for a moment, trying to get his breathing evened out. After a minute or so, he turned and started the shower. Pushing his boxers to the floor, he stepped into the stinging spray—sling and all. He could throw it in the dryer later. But when he closed his eyes, it all came rushing back.

He had been having the best dream. Trace had him pinned facedown on the bed, his face buried in the fleshy crook between David's shoulder and neck, his dark, sweet-smelling hair spilling over them as his lean body arched, his cock sliding slowly in and pulling even more slowly out of David in steady, rhythmic glides. David pushed his ass back onto his lover, mumbling a quiet plea for more into the sheet-covered padding.

"Mmm. Yes... Trace," David had moaned, pushing his ass toward the hard cock that rocked in and out of him.

David's body had rolled to the right to give his lover better access—and he had glanced his broken shoulder against the stack of firm pillows. With a jolt of sharp pain, he had snapped wide awake. Horrified, he had practically jumped away from Trace's sleep-warm body, jarring his shoulder again and clenching his teeth to keep from crying out. Panting, he had slung his legs over the side of the bed and hurried into the safety of the bathroom.

Letting the water sluice over his body, he couldn't seem to stop his hand from curling around his still half-hard cock. He groaned, squeezing, but still not fully committed to bringing himself off. There was just something about jacking off to thoughts of Trace fucking him that pushed him across an invisible line he wasn't sure he was ready to cross. Having Trace playing nursemaid was both the best and the worst thing that had ever happened to him.

Squeezing his eyes shut, David awkwardly added a palmful of shampoo to his hair, working it into a lather. As he rinsed the suds from his hair, his hand followed them down over his chest, his fingers running into the hair around his still-throbbing cock, and he gave in. Still slick, his fingers curled around the shaft and stroked, the awkwardness of using his left hand eased by the soap and frustration. His forehead came to rest against the cool sandstone wall as his hand shuttled up and down, images from his dream quickly pushing him over the edge. He gasped, whimpering as his cock pulsed in his hand. "Trace," he whispered desperately.

David's body shook with the force of his orgasm, and he stood with his left shoulder braced against the shower wall until the water had heated his skin enough for it to feel cool. Twisting the faucets to turn it off, he stepped out of the tub, his muscles feeling like wet noodles. Drying himself as best he could, he gingerly slipped the sling off, letting it fall onto the floor with a wet squelch. Then he remembered. *Damn.* He'd been in such a hurry to hide in the bathroom that he hadn't brought in any clean clothes. Peering out the bathroom door, he verified that Trace was still asleep before tiptoeing to the dresser and pulling open a drawer to find a clean pair of boxers and sweatpants.

The sounds of the drawers pulling open shook Trace from sleep, and he turned his head, lifting up a bit and mumbling, "David? Izzat you?"

Jumping guiltily, David looked back over his shoulder, sure Trace would be able to read everything in his face. Clutching the folded clothes to his crotch, he walked back toward the bathroom, keeping his back to the bed. "Ah, yeah, just grabbing clean clothes. Go back to sleep."

"'kay," Trace said sleepily, shifting to bury his face back in the pillow, just one drowsy eye staying open and training on David for a moment before drooping closed. Safely hidden in the bathroom,

David looked out the mostly closed door at the dozing man. How was it possible for one man to be so erotically tempting and cuddly cute at the same time? With a sigh, he quietly shut the door.

ABOUT two hours or so later, Trace walked out to the kitchen wearing his suit pants and dark socks with just an undershirt. His damp hair was pulled back into a neat tail at the nape of his neck. He opened the fridge and pulled out the juice, pouring himself a glass. "Morning," he mumbled, still sleepy and grumpy despite his shower. He was *not* a morning person.

David stared at the jug sitting next to Trace's hand on the counter. He never kept orange juice in the house. He didn't like it. But with Trace doing all of the shopping now, the contents of the refrigerator were a mix of both men's favorites. It was both comforting and alarming at the same time.

"Morning, sleepyhead," David teased, hitting save on his laptop. His writing had slowed down considerably with only one hand, but at least he had the kind of job he could do from home in a pinch. And missing Monday morning editorial meetings wasn't necessarily a bad thing.

Sliding the bottle of juice back in the fridge, Trace pulled English muffins out of the cabinet and popped one into the toaster. "Want a muffin?" he asked sleepily as he got butter and a knife out after a long minute of staring at the sink.

"I had one of those premixed omelets when I got up," David said, forcing his eyes back to his computer screen. "So, into the office today?"

Trace dropped the toasted muffin onto a paper towel and fixed it up as he muttered to himself before answering "Yeah" a little louder. He brought the glass and the muffin to the table with a yawn, sitting down across from David. "Gotta work on the Readers'

Choice restaurant reviews. I won't be home for dinner." He took a bite of muffin and chewed, head propped in one hand, eyes closed again.

He won't be home for dinner. Home. David blinked away the dangerous thoughts. "I imagine I'll survive. Where are you reviewing tonight?" He got up and retrieved the strawberry jam from the refrigerator, snagging a spoon out of the drainer. Setting it down next to his sleepy friend, he realized that he knew Trace's preferences almost as well as Trace knew his.

Trace heard the clink of the jar hit the table and opened his eyes, brightening at seeing the jam. He pushed the split muffin over for some. "Kabuki uptown, Raffi's on Highstreet, and Delectable, the new dessert place. I'm gonna be a whale when I get done. I really ought to make them spread these reservations out more. I start at five and probably won't be done until eleven or later."

"Awwww. It's rough, but someone has to sacrifice and consume all those gourmet meals for free," David answered, carefully spreading a thin layer of jam on both halves of the muffin with the spoon in his left hand.

Trace sighed. "Yeah, and I'll have to spend an extra couple of hours at the gym to offset the calories. Thank God they only do this every other year."

Images of Trace half-naked and sweaty swam through David's mind. It was a familiar vision that now carried a different, more heated connotation. Shoving it firmly aside, he pushed the muffin back toward Trace, grabbed his mug, and went to pour himself another cup of coffee. Out of habit, he reached for the sugar with his right hand and yelped.

"David," Trace whined, "have some respect for the half-asleep, would you?" He shifted to look over at the other man and frowned. "Where's your sling?" he asked suspiciously.

"Ahh, well," David stammered nervously. "I sort of got it wet in the shower. It's still in the bathroom. Right after breakfast, I'm going to put it in the washer."

Trace raised an eyebrow and squinted his eyes in disapproval. "Sit your ass down, mister," he ordered as he stood up and headed back to the bathroom. Looking around, he found it on the floor against the cabinet; he'd missed it when he'd taken his shower. He wrung it out as best he could and took it straight to the dryer before heading back to the kitchen to cross his arms and shake his head at David.

David bit his tongue to keep from defending himself. He was a grown man, for fuck's sake. If he wanted to go without the blasted sling, he could do it. He couldn't tell if Trace was angry or disappointed, but either way, he felt like he had to explain. "I tried to keep it dry, but the soap slipped and...." He couldn't very well tell Trace why the soap slipped or what he was doing at the time. Fuck, he was an awful liar. "I tried. Honest."

Sighing, Trace walked over. "Why didn't you wake me?" he asked in concern. "I would have helped. That's why I'm here, David. I'm sorry if it feels like I'm mother-henning you. I'm just worried. I know it's hard for you to do things left-handed."

After running his fingers through his hair, David massaged the knotted muscles in his neck. "I just feel so blasted useless. I can't even do up my own jeans. I appreciate everything you're doing, really I do. I guess I'm just feeling too dependent."

"All right," Trace said soothingly, moving to lightly pull David's hand away and replace it with his own fingers, rubbing at the twisted tendons. "It's only been about a week, and you can't just start using that shoulder again so fast. But we'll work on getting you better, okay?"

"Okay." David hummed. "That feels really good." He swayed closer, his forehead dropping to rest on Trace's belly as the strong arms wrapped around him to massage his neck. It was true that he was tired of being weak—tired of being limited—but he wasn't tired of Trace being around. In fact, he was getting sort of used to it. Maybe too much.

"Your neck's a mess, probably from favoring your shoulder," Trace murmured. "And not wearing your sling won't help, either," he poked gently. "I know you're sick to death of it. I don't remember you ever being laid up this long before."

"Guess it just comes from getting old." David laughed quietly, relaxing even further into the incredible touch, ignoring that it brought him that much closer to Trace. "When I was younger I fell a lot harder than that while stumbling around drunk and never got hurt once."

"I told you before. You're not old," Trace insisted, kneading the softening muscles. "How you can be so self-deprecating and self-confident at the same time is a mystery to me."

David sighed. "I think it was the birthday." Trace had taken him to a weekend series of baseball games, and they'd had a great time. But the birthday itself....

"This past birthday?" Trace asked, frowning. He'd thought David had really enjoyed the weekend at the ballpark.

"None of my other birthdays have bothered me, but forty-five? That was the year my dad had his heart attack. He lived another ten years, but he was never the same."

Trace was quiet for a long moment. "That's not going to happen to you. Not as long as I'm around," he said seriously. "I'll make you exercise with me and eat better." He was determined. "Gotta take care of my best buddy, right?"

"Yeah." David grinned. "In the meantime, you've got to get to work, and I need to placate Lloyd with something printable. I promise, I'll be good and wear my sling," he said, sitting back, moving away from the soothing touch reluctantly.

Stepping back, Trace smiled at him. "All right. I hope to be home by ten tonight, although I'll need a forklift to move." He turned and walked out, back to the office where he'd taken to hanging his dry cleaning every few days. David had even cleaned some shelves off inside it for him.

David refilled his coffee cup and sat back down at the table to wait for his sling to dry. Pulling his laptop closer, he stared at the screen, trying to recapture where he'd been going with his column.

IT WAS later than he'd intended when Trace dragged himself out of the car and walked up to the house, leather case hanging from one shoulder, jacket slung over it, a small box in the other hand. He juggled it all to lift his keys and get the back door open, entering the kitchen quietly just in case David was asleep. The kitchen was dark, so he set his stuff on the table and put the box in the fridge before moving to stand in the doorway to the living room. As he walked he dragged a hand through his hair—it was hanging loose around his face. His shirt was open, with a triangle of his white undershirt showing, the tie hanging loose from the collar.

David was sitting on the couch with his laptop. "Hey," Trace greeted, leaning against the door frame.

David looked over his shoulder. "Oh, hey," he answered in a slightly dazed voice that showed he'd been deeply engrossed in something. "How was dinner?" Rubbing his eyes, he looked up at the clock. "Damn, it's late."

"Filling. Very, very filling," Trace answered, wrapping his arms around his midsection. "I brought you a piece of the richest cheesecake in creation," he added, knowing it was one of David's favorite treats.

"Really?" David asked, perking up. He'd been half-asleep, telling himself that he wasn't waiting up for Trace, but at the mention of cheesecake, he was wide awake. "Guess I have to make coffee, then," David added. "Can't have a good cheesecake without French roast."

Trace made a face. "No more food or liquids of any kind for at least twelve hours," he muttered, turning back into the kitchen and going to start the coffeemaker. It occurred to him that he hadn't even thought about bringing the cheesecake back; he'd just done it, knowing David would enjoy it. It was just a little thing—nothing like upsetting his whole life and moving in here to babysit him. Which honestly hadn't been upsetting at all, now that he thought about it.

David looked at the retreating back and grinned. It was the little things Trace did that made him so special. He remembered lots of times when Trace had brought him a bottle of wine or something local back from a business trip or called him when they'd both been busy and hadn't seen each other for a few weeks. Trace was just a great friend. And now, cheesecake!

"Come in here and talk to me," Trace called out as he measured the coffee. "I spent all night being stared at by wait staff."

"You got it." David strolled in and pulled a dessert plate off one of the shelves.

Trace frowned while watching him. *Why bother with a plate?*

Apparently David could read his mind. "What?" David said defensively. "A good dessert deserves first-class treatment, not to be shoveled out of a Styrofoam container."

Trace snorted. "I ate off fine Limoges china tonight, and believe me, sometimes it doesn't help." He shook his head, hitting the button to start the coffee brewing before turning and flopping in a chair at the table. "Oh God. *Kill* me now."

"You want some antacid?"

"I want a stomach pump," Trace muttered, head tilted against the back of the chair. "The food was pretty good, really. There was just way too much of it."

"You don't have to eat all of it, you know. Most critics just sample a few mouthfuls of each dish." David checked the coffeemaker. The cheesecake sitting in front of him was so tempting that it occurred to him he hadn't really eaten dinner. No wonder he was starved.

"Oh, believe me, that's all I do. Thing is, with these fancy restaurants, they bring you course after course after course—and even two or three bites adds up." Trace shifted on the chair. "I think I'll just explode right here. It'll be easier to clean the tile than the carpet."

"I'd rather you not explode anywhere in my house if it's just the same with you." David sighed as the light on the coffeemaker lit up. "*Finally.*"

Trace looked over, amused. It hadn't even been five minutes. "I swear, I think you love that coffee more than the cheesecake."

David grinned. "It's a mutual love affair. Each makes the other better." Slipping the first forkful of cheesecake into his mouth, he closed his lips around it, his eyes shut in orgasmic bliss. "Mmmmm...."

Trace chuckled. "See, I know how to turn you into a big pussy cat," he said with a smile. "Who else knows that?"

"Might be better than sex," David murmured, taking a sip of his coffee. "Will you marry me?"

"I don't know. You're awful difficult to live with," Trace said with a wink. "Although I like your house a hell of a lot more than my apartment." He toed out of his shoes, leaving them under the table, and got up to grab a bottle of water out of the fridge.

"Well, you know, high-maintenance partners are the best lovers," David teased back.

Trace turned around and leered at him. "High maintenance, are we?" he drawled. "My, my, really opening up now, aren't we? I'll have you know I have never had any complaints."

David chuckled, a low seductive sound, one Trace suspected was prompted by the late hour and really choice cheesecake. "If we were playing poker, I'd call."

Trace grinned, amazed at the sex just dripping from David's voice. It was like nothing he'd ever heard from his friend, and he surprised himself by shivering as a shot of heat buzzed through him. "Good thing we're not, 'cause I suck at bluffing," he said, screwing the top off the water bottle and taking a drink before sighing gustily. "No food until three p.m. tomorrow, I swear to God," he muttered.

"Poor baby," David purred before laughing. "How many restaurants do you have tomorrow night?"

Trace covered his face with both hands and moaned. "Three more." He made a mock-sobbing noise, only to look up and not see any sympathy from David. In fact, David was going at the cheesecake like a starving man. "Hey, I know you love cheesecake, but you eat that much sugar that fast, you'll be the one who's sick."

"I might have forgotten to eat dinner," David admitted, putting the fork down long enough to take a sip of coffee.

Trace's eyes narrowed. "Might have forgotten? I'm betting you remember one way or the other."

David's eyes shifted guiltily to the floor. "I ate lunch," he justified.

Glancing at the clock, Trace closed his eyes for a moment and restrained himself. *Why can't David take better care of himself?* He leaned back on the counter, hands clenching on the edge as he swallowed the urge to get angry, and made a decision. "Okay. Well, you just solved one of my problems," he said, keeping his voice deceptively casual despite the unhappy bent to his shoulders.

Confused, David stared at Trace, brows drawn together. "Huh?"

Trace pushed himself away from the counter and walked over to David, setting one hand on the table and one on the back of David's chair. He leaned down close to meet David's eyes. "I'm taking you out and wining and dining you tomorrow night."

A shiver traveled up David's spine, even though he knew that Trace didn't mean it the way it sounded. An unexpected pang that Trace wasn't actually asking him out shot through David's gut. To regain his balance, he teased back. "Sure you can afford me?"

"Oh, tomorrow night, money is no object. Caviar and champagne, filet mignon and crusted Australian bass, lobster bisque and duck salad, scallop crostini, French vanilla crème brûlée…. Whatever your little heart desires, you can have," Trace said, his voice smooth and dark, like velvet. Trace knew he was having an effect when David swallowed audibly and nodded.

David shivered again. Cheesecake and a seductive Trace were more than his system could handle. Unable to tear his eyes away from the chocolate gaze, he gulped, nodding because he didn't trust his voice.

"Oh yeah, baby," Trace crooned, leaning closer. "You are going to all three restaurants with me. I'll make sure you eat. And you'll love every… single… succulent… moment of it."

"Enough, Trace. I'll go. Now go sit down like a good little straight boy before I jump you," David warned, his tone dark, but still teasing.

Trace grinned and leaned just enough to playfully kiss the very tip of David's nose before standing up and moving back to the other side of the table, water bottle in hand. He sat down, smug and very pleased with himself. And he was: This meant that not only would he have David's wonderful company instead of nervous waiters, but he'd only have to eat half as much food! *Why didn't I think of this before?*

• Chapter 5

DAVID looked at himself in the mirror. His black linen pants were drawn up over his hips but not fastened. He'd gotten his undershirt on and his shirt over his shoulders without too much trouble, although it had hurt to move his shoulder around that much. Of course, the buttons weren't done. He *could* do them up, but one-handed it would take the next hour at least, and it still hurt a lot when he tried hold his right arm up long enough to use it. So, he was as ready as he was going to get. Taking a deep breath, he called, "Oh, Trace, I need my valet!"

He heard a bark of laughter from the bathroom, and, rolling his eyes, David fixed his glare on the bathroom door so that Trace would feel its full impact when he walked through. The glare, and his breathing, faltered when Trace appeared.

Fuck. Trace was good-looking at his worst, but dressed to kill, he was breathtaking. Unable to form a coherent comment, David just stared as his friend walked toward him. It was a similar feeling to sitting at the table last night, Trace's voice rubbing him silkily in all the right places, leaving him aching.

Trace had broken out more than the run-of-the-mill everyday dress clothes, choosing a silvery-gray suit of lighter material that emphasized the long, lean lines of his body, and his hair was loose and on his shoulders, styled in that popular windblown look and held in place with judicious use of mousse. He'd even shaved again this evening.

Looking over at David, Trace raised a brow. "Oh Master, I heed thy summons," he said with a chuckle.

David's glare didn't faze Trace one bit; he'd seen it before and would see it again, he was sure. He sauntered over and stopped in front of David, starting to button his shirt from the top down, smoothing the fine white fabric as he went. It was hard to miss the lightly muscled body underneath, and Trace was quietly appreciative. He knew it took a lot to stay in shape. He could certainly appreciate the effect on David's body.

Trace tucked the shirttails into David's slacks, hands coasting over his hips to make sure the material didn't bunch. Trace looked up as he pulled the pants up slightly and folded the placket together. "What's up? You look like you forgot something," he said as he buttoned the trousers.

Yeah, my brain. David wished he knew what had possessed him to think that Trace moving in with him while he recovered was a good idea. Of course, Trace hadn't really given him a choice in the matter. The corners of his mouth drew up slightly at how pigheaded and stubborn Trace could be when he set his mind to it. David bit his cheek, willing his body to behave as Trace's long-fingered hands skimmed his body.

David really needed to get laid. But he couldn't see having a conversation with Trace about needing a night alone when Trace had done so much for him. He was quite sure, though, that his thoroughly straight friend wasn't going to want to do what David really needed at the moment.

He shook his head in answer to Trace's question and looked down to watch as Trace buttoned, zipped, and buckled him up.

"There you go," Trace said as he slid his hand along David's belly to make sure the shirt lay down properly.

David swallowed hard, not sure how much more of this he could take. It was becoming torture.

Trace lifted his hands to fasten the top button under his chin. "Wearing a tie?" he asked. His own was the same silver as the suit, and it caught the light when he moved.

"Yeah. If you're gonna button me up like a priest, I'd better," David managed to say drolly.

Trace chuckled. "You can go without one; no one's going to say anything. Will look nicer if your gossip columnist catches us, though. Did you know Matt's been haunting the high-class places for Katherine's celebrity column? He got a shot of me last night talking with the deputy mayor and her husband. I hope he doesn't use it, or at least crops me out. I probably looked like shit after twelve hours on the job."

"You could never look like shit, fashion plate that you are. Fine. Just for you, I'll try and look my best," David teased—but not really—and looked at Trace coyly through lowered eyelashes.

With an appraising look, Trace stepped back and deliberately looked David up and down. There was no doubt, David was a fine-looking man. Trace supposed he had no problem finding companionship when he went out. "Well, I'm no expert—about men, anyway—but you look incredible to me," he admitted as he tilted his head and started to fix the tie David laid over his shoulder.

Trace's plain brown eyes were sparkling unusually as he stepped to one side to playfully peek at David's ass. The tease on top of the "incredible" comment was the ice water David needed to get his rampaging libido under control. Trace wasn't gay, and David hadn't actively lusted after straight men in almost two decades; it was far too frustrating. "Thank you," he said stiffly, slipping the sling over the top of his suit coat and fiddling with the strap to lengthen it to accommodate the extra bulk. "I don't suppose you'd let me out without the leash just for one night?" he grumbled.

Stepping back to let David move, Trace slid one hand into a pocket. David had stiffened a bit, and Trace realized maybe he'd teased a little too much. He'd have to pick it apart in his head later, try and figure it out. As for the sling…. "I won't give you grief about it, not tonight. I'm just afraid you'll be hurting if you don't wear it," he said quietly.

David sighed over the thought of a few hours without the frustrating contraption. "How about a compromise? I'll take it, leave it in the car, and if I get to hurting, I'll let you go get it for me."

Trace chuckled. "I suppose I can live with that." He shrugged into his jacket and glanced at his watch. "Ready to go? We've got half an hour to get to the restaurant."

Pulling aside his suit coat to slip his wallet into his back pocket, and his money clip and a small tin of mints into his front pocket, David motioned to the door. "All set. After you."

DAVID gritted his teeth. The hostess at San Angelo hadn't stopped flirting, fawning, and gushing over Trace since he and David had walked in the door. She currently had her hand wrapped around Trace's bicep, squeezing like she was testing the condition of the body beneath the expensive suit. Judging by her smile, she liked what she'd found. David wondered if restaurant staff thought they could use sex to influence the overall rating of a restaurant in the *Sun-Herald* reviews. He was so caught up in his inner grumbling that he reached to pull out the heavy mahogany chair with his right hand without thinking, yanking it back from the table and unable to completely stifle the cry of pain.

Trace's head shot around, and he was at David's side in an instant, leaving the hostess gaping. "David, what did you do?" he asked, looking at how David was cradling his arm to prop up his shoulder.

David stared at a fixed point, trying to keep his balance as the room swayed. "Just being stupid. How about being a gentleman and pulling out my chair for me? I don't seem to be capable of it at the moment."

Concerned, Trace did pull out the heavy wooden chair, immediately aware of how it must have hurt David to move it. He totally ignored the hostess and wait staff staring. Once David was seated, he asked, "Okay?" and when David nodded, he pushed the chair in some. "You can probably prop your elbow on that armrest," he suggested, moving to the chair across the two-person table.

David was watching the befuddled young woman hover with two heavy, leather-bound menus and an even fatter wine list, backed up by two nervous-looking servers. "I'm fine. Just give me a sec," he whispered. "Do something about them hovering, will you? I feel like a wounded gazelle being eyed by a leopard."

Trace accepted the menus and the wine list and made a blatant shooing motion at the wait staff. Scared to death of damaging his opinion, they all vamoosed. He set down the menus on the table, one in front of each of them, and looked at David with concern.

"Quit staring." David glanced up from the menu that lay open in front of him. "I just wasn't thinking and grabbed the chair. Give me a second, and I'll be fine. Now, what do I need to order or do you want to order for me too? After pulling out my chair, we could really get some rumors flying." David glanced up coyly and fluttered his eyelashes.

Trace blinked and smiled at David's good mood. "Order whatever you like. I'll get different things so we have a selection." He toyed with the wine list. "Rumors, huh? About you or about me?" he asked, lips twitching. "I'm sure it won't be long before someone recognizes you and wonders why we're out together."

"Yeah. Lloyd'll give me hell. As for rumors, it is far more fun to speculate about a couple than an individual, and I was only half-joking. If it'll bother you, we need to make sure we present the proper 'friends out on the town comparing conquests' front." David closed his menu and laid it to the side. "I'm having seafood."

Trace supposed the chance of rumors wasn't so unbelievable. He took a few moments to muse over that, but he decided it didn't bother him. They were best friends. Rumors of romance wouldn't change it; he didn't feel uncomfortable at all around David. He'd never felt uncomfortable before, so there was no reason for that to change.

Trace's voice was serious and low when he spoke. "It doesn't bother me, David. Not at all. I'm out with a hell of a good-looking man. Why should I complain?" Trace closed his menu. "I'll have the mixed grill."

"You might want to reconsider. Matt just walked in the door with that young freelance photographer who's been hot lately. Being paired with a man, no matter how good-looking, can put a serious crimp in your ability to attract women," David warned, opening the wine list and doing his best to ignore the two men being seated three tables away. It wasn't that he had anything against Matt. They were actually good friends. The man took beautiful pictures, but he did have a tendency to take everything to an extreme. And if he was filling in as a photographer for Katherine's gossip column, he'd be looking for good gossip.

"I'm not worried about it," Trace said. The thought of being paired with David didn't cause any internal conflict other than a warm feeling that he could possibly attribute to amusement and definitely associate to their close friendship. Now, that being said, it did occur to Trace that while taking care of David, helping him up off the bathroom floor that time, doing up his dress pants, and buttoning the fly of David's close-fitting jeans, he simply hadn't applied the thought of David's fetching appearance in any terms to himself. Until now.

"How about this?" Trace suggested. "If it gets to be a problem, I'll call up a couple or three gorgeous girlfriends of mine and go to some high-profile event, okay? Aren't you concerned about your own reputation?"

David shrugged. "Let's just say that Matt is aware of my orientation, and I trust him not to do anything to hurt me."

Trace nodded slowly. "So that's why you're concerned that he might put something out there about me. Especially since I work at the *Herald*?"

"I can promise he'll be honest, but he only contributes the pictures. Katherine's the one who will add the words. I personally think the rivalry is crap. This area is by far big enough to support two dailies, but...." David shrugged again. "You know how it is. I also know that Katherine bid on you and lost at the hospital benefit last year. She didn't lose gracefully."

"Mmmm, I forgot about that," Trace admitted, remembering the fuss.

They were interrupted as the waiter arrived to take their orders, obviously having been told to be ultra-attentive and polite. Finally he left as another server arrived with before-dinner drinks and ice water. Once they were left in relative peace, Trace picked up the discussion again. "So, why didn't she win?"

David smirked. "Well, let's say she had been a cocky bitch all week about wanting you, and a few of us might have decided to distract her at a key moment."

Trace's brows rose in disbelief. "You did *what*? Most of the crew from your paper were hootin' and hollerin' while I was up there, trying to embarrass me. Who helped you?"

"Well, actually, Matt and the sports editor, Chad. We were pretty drunk and feeling devious." David grinned, his eyes turning soft and crinkling around the corners at the memory. It had been a fun night. Trace's hadn't been the only auction they'd influenced. They'd given Keri Carter from copy a thousand dollars to bid on Bill Winchell, and those two were still dating.

It had been a fun night, Trace remembered. Shaking his head, he smiled at the man across the table. "You are a true friend. I shudder to think what Katherine would have wanted."

"Ha!" David barked. "I can tell you exactly what she would have wanted. Her business is rumors, and she'd heard exactly how good you are with that tongue of yours."

Oh my fucking God! Trace's eyes bulged and he leaned back, jaw dropping. "You're *joking!*"

David's laughter got worse when he saw the expression on Trace's face, and tears of mirth filled his eyes. "No."

Just then the couple was interrupted by Matt's amiable appearance at their table, his companion left behind at his table. "David, you should wait for dinner to arrive before hitting the really hard spirits," Matt teased, smiling indulgently while David tried valiantly to quit laughing.

"Sorry," David gasped, his shoulders still shaking. He brushed the tears away from his eyes. "I just.... Well, Trace...." He broke into a new gale of laughter.

Matt turned to Trace and extended his hand. "I guess I'll try talking to you. He doesn't seem too coherent. If part of your game plan is getting him drunk, I'd say you are well on your way," he added in good humor. "I'm Matt Hardwick."

Trace shook Matt's hand, still aghast. "Trace Jackson. I might have to cut him off if he keeps sharing things I certainly don't want to hear. Dear *God.* I had no idea Katherine would hear about something like that!"

Understanding bloomed on Matt's face. "Oh." He snickered, not looking at David as he tried to keep his amusement under control. "Yeah, you should never underestimate Katherine." Finally turning to David, he said, "What have you been telling him?"

Hiccupping, David tried to pull himself together. "Sorry. He just asked about Katherine, and... God! I keep seeing this image of

Katherine's face on a spider's body with Trace caught firmly in her web... do you remember the look on her face when she lost?" The laughter started again.

Matt smiled and laughed along. "Yeah, that was classic. So, are you sharing secrets with the enemy?" He cuffed David's shoulder lightly, inadvertently causing David to wince and jerk away into the high back of the chair, which was even worse.

"Be careful," Trace warned. "David... hurt his shoulder," he said, not sure what Lloyd might have told the other employees.

Matt's smile faded with concern. "I'm sorry," he said, but then the smirk was back, and his serious tone turned teasing again as he added, "I've warned you about wrenching around when you're handcuffed to the bed."

"Fucker!" David shot back, eyes crinkling as he struck out at Matt with his good arm. "Go back to your boy toy and leave us men alone."

Trace covered his mouth one-handed, his elbow on the table, stifling the spate of laughter he'd been half-choking on since David's description of Katherine. He considered admitting that he'd thought about something along those lines—tying David down to keep him in the damn bed to give his shoulder a rest—but he was sure that would definitely come out sounding wrong. And Matt had a boy toy? Trace glanced over at the younger man, who looked like he should be a model, and back to Matt, raising a brow in question.

Matt leaned low, whispering something in David's ear that made his eyes lower and his cheeks bloom with color. With a careful pat of David's back, Matt moved away, glancing back at their table once speculatively.

"Oh, I'm never going to hear the end of this one," David predicted, lifting his glass of water to his lips.

Eyebrow still raised, Trace sighed and leaned back in his chair. "Do I even want to know?" he asked as he lifted his drink.

"Probably not," David confirmed. "Matt and I go way back, and not all of that history would be suitable for polite conversation."

Trace snorted. "And my tongue is polite conversation?" He rolled his eyes as the waiter appeared with fresh salads and their appetizer.

David lifted his fork, still awkward with his left hand. "Let's just say this history includes some moments of an intimate nature that would include body parts *you* usually don't deal with outside of your own shower." As soon as he said the words, images of Trace naked and soapy ran through his mind, taking the edge off his physical hunger, but raising a hunger of an entirely different kind.

"Gotcha," Trace said. He picked up a crostino topped with tomato and cheese and tilted his head to pop the bite-size morsel in his mouth. "Mmmm. This gets an A," he said while chewing happily.

"You are entirely too easy to please for a restaurant critic." David chuckled.

"I'll have you know, my average review is two and a quarter stars out of four," Trace said archly, smiling smugly when the manager who had been approaching the table blanched and scurried away.

David snorted, shaking his head. "You just gave that man nightmares."

Trace raised an eyebrow and shrugged. "Maybe they'll triple-check the food, then." He smiled, leaning back and lifting his drink. "To a wonderful first dinner," he toasted.

Something warm settled in David's belly that had nothing to do with the wine. Raising his glass, he touched Trace's with a delicate clink. "If I forget to tell you later—thank you." David's blue eyes stayed locked with Trace's as he drank slowly, his tongue peeking out to touch the edge of the glass before pulling the wine into his mouth.

A slow tingle flowed through Trace as he watched David take the sip of wine, and he blinked several times, trying to recognize it before it was gone. Was all the teasing making him think about things—about David—in a way he normally wouldn't? David's eyes—had he ever noticed they were so blue and flecked with gold? He swallowed his wine and dropped his eyes, feeling a tinge of heat in his cheeks.

Trace took a couple of small bites of the salad and pushed it aside, dismissing it as standard fare, and instead nipped another crostino from the plate. He didn't know why he felt nervous all of a sudden. This was David, his best friend of a few years now. Finally, it occurred to him. He had just realized that he actually saw David as a handsome man, not just as his best friend who happened to be a guy who happened to look good. "You're welcome," he said quietly, glancing up at David, finding that he was still struck by how the light from the small flickering candle transformed David's eyes.

Snagging the last of the crostini from the plate, David grinned as the sharp taste of plum tomatoes and garlic exploded in his mouth. "God, tell me that when I'm cursing you later. Do we have Alka-Seltzer at home?"

Chuckling, Trace nodded. "Yeah, I had some last night." He relaxed again with the easy comment, and it was easy to smile now. "So you think you might be able to suffer through the rest of the night?"

David's reply was stalled by the arrival of a tray of steaming, aromatic food, David shot an amused glance at Trace when the manager personally served their dinner. As Trace dismissed the fawning man gracefully, David rolled his eyes and said, "It'll be rough, but I think I'll manage."

• Chapter 6

TRACE drove along the winding lane that led back into town, his long hair ruffled by the wind. Keeping the top down had been an excellent idea, even if they'd had to spike the heat to stay comfortable. They were heading home from the exclusive French restaurant they'd visited to end the evening, and this time, he was pleasantly full, not ill like the previous night.

They had just dined at La Vie en Rose, outside on a terrace, the table furnished with china, silver, crystal, and linen—definitely a very romantic atmosphere—and the food had been unbelievable. Even to his experienced tastes. Totally worth his ultra-rare four-star designation.

Trace felt no shame at all in pressing David to share his opinions about the food. He glanced over at the man in the passenger seat. "So what'd you think about that one?"

David's head rolled lethargically to the side so he could see Trace. "Definitely a 'sure thing' kind of place."

A huge grin split Trace's face, and he tried to bite his tongue. But it was so easy. "You telling me you're a sure thing?"

"Trace, if I thought you had any inclination, I'd let you fuck me through the mattress," David murmured in a sleepy, sated voice, his eyes already closed, the wind whipping through his short hair as he drifted off to sleep, lulled by the rich food, good wine, and steady vibration of the convertible.

Trace froze with both hands on the steering wheel, looking straight out at the road. But he wasn't seeing it. His mind exploded with visions of what David had just said, and he had to swallow hard and blink to make sure he was watching where he was driving. *What the…?*

He chanced a look in David's direction and let out a long, shaky breath. After the first meal, when he'd met Matt—perhaps stemming from the totally not-for-polite-company conversation about his *tongue*—the evening had been rife with a simmering tension Trace had never felt around David before. And he had enjoyed it. He shifted in the seat uncomfortably, and a few moments after the fact he realized why. He was aroused. Terribly, undeniably aroused by the images David's words had evoked. He dragged a hand through his hair, some odd sort of panic welling in his throat. His hand moved to cover his mouth as he choked on a scared laugh. *What the hell?*

With time, the grace of God, and sheer willpower, Trace calmed just as he pulled into David's driveway. Common sense had taken over. David was exhausted and probably more than a little drunk—and on painkillers to boot. *Drugs make you do and say crazy things, right?* And the concepts had at least already been in Trace's own mind after that meet-up with Matt. Perhaps David was just free-associating, but… he'd made it clear he knew who he was talking to. But David knew Trace was straight and happy that way, so surely it was just a flip, throwaway comment between friends, meant to be funny, meant to be a joke they could laugh over later. Trace sighed and open the car door, dropping one leg out and leaning back in his seat to look up at the starry sky.

If the idea bothered him this much, it looked like he had quite a bit of thinking to do. Trace wasn't one for hiding things from himself, and he never lied to himself.

Fingers tapping lightly on the steering wheel, after a bit Trace shifted to spend quite a few minutes just looking at David, studying him like he'd never thought to before. Admittedly, he hadn't been kidding when he made his claim about being out with a hell of a good-looking man. Trace had no problem saying which men looked better than others, in his opinion. The more he thought about it, he wondered how much his opinions had been unconsciously formed with David as the benchmark.

Finally Trace reached over, intending to shake David's arm, but instead his fingers moved to the soft blond hair, and he petted it on purpose, just to feel—not to make a point, not to give comfort, but just because he wanted to. After more than a few heartbeats he drew back, blinking in confusion. *David wouldn't appreciate that, would he?* Still curious, Trace reached out again to comb his fingers through the wind-ruffled hair again, wondering if it would wake him.

David's head turned on the headrest, pressing into the gentle touch without waking. His lashes fluttered momentarily before he settled back into sleep, his lips parting as his jaw relaxed. Trace leaned sideways against his seat, head pillowed against the leather as he gazed across the two feet to his hand sliding through golden hair, and he smiled softly as David relaxed. To be so trusted, it was something special, he knew. He sighed, carefully pulling his hand away and touching his friend's lower arm. "David," he said quietly. "We're home."

David's mind reluctantly emerged from sleep. *Someone is stroking my hair.* It had been a long time since he'd enjoyed such a simple, intimate touch. He was loath to open his eyes and have it end. He could smell the subtle tang of Trace's cologne and the combination of scent and touch made his pulse pick up. He slowly opened his eyes, adding the image of his friend's beautiful face, lit by moonlight, to his fantasy. David held his breath, caught in the magnetic pull of the moment.

Clear blue eyes opened, and Trace felt a flutter in his chest, one he didn't recognize but somehow knew was important. The corner of his mouth turned up. "Wake up, sleeping beauty. We're home," he said softly.

For a moment, still foggy with good food, good wine, and the warmth of Trace's touch, David let himself hear the words as a lover would say them. *Home*. Not David's home, but theirs. A place of love. A promise of making love once they were safely ensconced in the privacy of their bedroom. A tight burning knot formed in his stomach as he imagined Trace's eyes turned to melted chocolate by arousal and love.

Swallowing and licking his lips to ease the dryness, David straightened and tried to shake off the appealing vision. "Yeah. My shoulder hurts. Probably should pop some more pills and go to bed," he murmured, the words a reminder to himself of why Trace was here.

Trace seemed to pause a few moments before pulling his fingers away, leaving David immediately missing the warmth. "Let's go, then," he murmured.

David recognized that he didn't want to move away, but he shifted out of his seat to stand regardless. Now wasn't the time to go exploring crazy feelings inspired by an oddly romantic night out with his best friend. He shook himself slightly and closed the car door.

Without waiting for Trace, David got out of the car and headed up the path to the front door, hoping to buy himself a few seconds alone to compose himself. He struggled inserting the key with his left hand, cursing in frustration when he dropped the keys. "Goddamn it! Fucking idiot." Slamming his palm against the wooden door, he rested his forehead against the beveled glass inset and took several calming breaths. He hated feeling incompetent, and he hated feeling shaken even more.

Trace stood back, even though he wanted to step up and help. David had become increasingly unhappy with being coddled, and Trace now had to admit that he should probably be thinking about going home before David threw him out in annoyance. "Okay?" Trace ventured.

"Fine," David ground out from between clenched teeth. Taking another deep breath, he leaned over and retrieved the keys, unsure if it was being forced to use his left hand or Trace standing so close that was making him tremble. Finally on the third try, he got the key inserted in the lock and turned. It was a small victory, but he'd take what he could get.

Standing in the hall, David looked from the hallway leading to the bedroom to the comfortable living room. He wasn't sure his control was up to Trace helping him undress just yet. "How about a drink now that you aren't worried about driving us home?" he suggested.

For whatever reason, David mentioning home made Trace feel warm all over and a little on the shaky side. And he hadn't touched a drop of alcohol, whereas David had been drinking quite a bit. "Sure," he said quietly. "Gonna break out the good stuff?" he asked as he shrugged out of his suit jacket and loosened his tie. Maybe a drink would help him settle what he'd considered in the car.

"You're worth nothing less." David walked over to the cabinet and pulled an unmarked dark bottle out of it. "Get us a couple of glasses," he suggested as he glanced up. He met Trace's eyes for a bare moment before Trace lowered his lashes and turned away. David's body reacted to the shy drop of Trace's eyes with a surge of desire; if he'd been out on a real date, he'd be sure that his companion was interested in him and probably thinking naughty thoughts. With Trace, he didn't know what to think. Their friendship was deepening in a way that felt different from anything he'd experienced before. Watching Trace leave the room, he worked on shedding his jacket and getting his body under control.

Trace walked into the kitchen and pulled two tumblers from the cabinet, stopping in the shadowed room for a moment to think. What had he been thinking of in the car? He looked down at his hands. Setting aside the glasses, Trace stepped to the sink and turned on the cold water, plunging his hands into it. He had to snap out of this. Yeah, it was definitely time for a night out, ending with a good lay. He was starting to fantasize about David! He sighed, turned off the water, dried his hands, picked up the glasses, and walked into the den. He'd think more about it later. Now, scotch. Lots of it.

Bolstered by his success at that much undressing on his own, David started to work on his tie, draping it over the back of the chair. Toeing off his shoes, he stretched out on the couch and propped his feet on the table, feeling accomplished for a change. Hearing the clink of glass, David bolstered his calm and smiled over his shoulder. "I've got a special treat for you. I found this bottle in a little pub in Scotland that didn't even have a sign outside."

David's first words sent a shiver through Trace. Maybe this wasn't such a good idea. A laid-back guy in general, Trace knew he got even more pliable and agreeable when drunk. He also tended to say things he otherwise wouldn't. "I'll try a bit," he said, planning to have a taste and then flee to the shower. Right now, just being around David at all was keeping him aroused. He should have calmed by now, he kept telling himself.

Taking the glasses from Trace's hands, David poured them both a drink. "Sit. Now close your eyes and take a sip."

Trace sat as instructed and accepted the glass, looking at David with a touch of amusement before closing his eyes and lifting the glass, letting just a tiny amount slip between his lips. He inhaled sharply as the flavor and intensity exploded across his tongue, and he swallowed once, then a second time.

"Incredible, isn't it?" David purred. Instead of following his own advice, his eyes were open as he savored the rich, smoky, smooth liquor and the memories of obtaining it. Hearing a soft moan, he peered at Trace to see his reaction to the drink.

Having taken another slightly larger sip, Trace sank back into the couch, eyes still closed, a rapturous look on his face as he slowly licked his bottom lip of the drop of scotch that had escaped. Watching Trace's tongue swipe across his lips, David felt the same irresistible pull he'd felt in the car. He wanted to lean over and lick the rich scotch off Trace's lips and tongue, but instead he took another drink and closed his eyes again, blocking out at least the visual temptation. Trace had taken off his jacket on his way into the kitchen, and his sprawl rumpled his shirt and tie just a little... just enough to be greatly appealing to David's eyes. He could still smell Trace's cologne, feel the warmth of his body, and hear the delicious sounds Trace was making as he enjoyed the scotch. *Surely that's enough.*

Trace sighed happily, took another few sips, and propped the glass on his knee. "Maybe I'll drink some more of this and sleep right here," he murmured lazily, sinking back into the corner of the sofa. A fuzzy warmth was already spreading, after just half a tumbler. It was easier now to discount his worries and odd reactions and difficult questions. Now he could just relax and... float. "David?" Trace asked, opening his eyes. "Do you need any help before I conk out? Because if I drink the rest of this glass and the second one I'm planning on, I won't be getting off this couch."

"Yeah, and you'll end up on the floor like you did that first night. Don't you remember how much trouble you had sleeping out here?" David reminded. He'd heard about it extensively at breakfast the next morning. It seemed so long ago now.

Pouring them both another glass, David stood up, and the words were out of his mouth before he could censor them. "Come on. Let's go to bed. I'll let you nursemaid me, we'll finish our scotch, and we can pass out in comfort." David shook his head and took another drink, a deeper draught than he should have. Luckily, the acute attraction he'd been feeling for Trace had mellowed a little with the alcohol, and as Trace stood, he was able to admire the curve of Trace's ass without feeling the need to push him against the wall and molest him. Too much.

71

Blinking a few times, Trace tried not to think about the possible double meaning behind what David had just said. *Let's go to bed.* Trace had honestly never given the idea any thought before, not between himself and David; it was like he was sensitized to it tonight. More scotch required. "Okay," he said, pushing himself up from the couch and picking up the bottle on his way to the bedroom.

David followed him as he stepped into the room and looked at the bed. Walking in front of him, Trace threw back the rest of his drink, gasping and gripping the door frame after swallowing it down. He dragged in a breath and cleared his throat before walking to the dresser, putting down the glass, and refilling it. The crazy night had really gotten to him. He started unbuttoning his shirt, looking at himself unsteadily in the mirror as the scotch visibly started to kick in.

David stood in the doorway watching as Trace started to undress. He'd seen Trace tipsy many, many times. It took a fair amount of alcohol, and David was tempted to take the rare bottle away from him and replace it with one from the corner liquor store, but that felt petty after everything Trace had done for him since he'd gotten hurt. Walking up behind his friend, David laid a hand on his shoulder and caught Trace's gaze in the mirror. "You okay?" he asked. Trace was downright gorgeous with his hair tumbled loose about his face. David had to swallow past the tightening in his throat as Trace's tanned muscular chest was revealed by the open shirt, but the expression on Trace's face was definitely not happy, and it cooled David's ardor.

Trace raised his eyes in the mirror to look back at David and tilted his head to one side, sending his hair coasting over one shoulder. He vaguely noted that David was disheveled. And it really looked good on him. "I'm abusing your scotch," he said apologetically.

David's eyes were riveted on Trace's reflection as he felt the heat from the liquor in his stomach spread to his chest and groin. He wondered if there could ever be any chance of Trace seeing him as he saw Trace. Seductively appealing. God, he felt hot. And Trace standing so close just made it worse.

The look in Trace's eyes softened, his face relaxing into a smile, and David's body heated in a way that had nothing to do with the scotch. Coughing to cover the needy moan that rose unbidden in his throat, David turned and started working on his own buttons one-handed. "Oh, um, that's okay. What's scotch for if not to drink?"

"Mmm. To savor? To sip and feel it burn its way down and up again until you're warm all over?" Trace drew out in a husky voice as he lifted the refilled glass. He was definitely drunk, but not so much so that he didn't know it. And Trace could tell his body was remembering how it had felt in the car, though his mind was a step behind.

Still looking back at David in the mirror—studying, maybe even staring—Trace watched David's lips move, and a question popped to mind unbidden: Would David's lips be soft and giving, molding against his? Or hard and unyielding like Trace imagined a man's were?

Trace's words spread through David like the scotch, warming him to an almost uncomfortable burn. His mind automatically converted the innocent description to images of Trace savoring and sipping him as he sank down to his knees in front of him....

Fuck! He should have left Trace on the couch. There was no way he was going to be able to hide his cock's very visceral reaction when he had to ask Trace for help. Most of his buttons were undone, but David had tried doing this belt one-handed before, and it just didn't work.

Without being asked, Trace set down the glass of scotch and walked over to David. First he reached out and finished unbuttoning David's shirt. He could feel the heat of David's body radiating. He hadn't felt it before. Trace pulled the shirt free of the waistband, and he accidentally brushed his fingertips along David's belly as he dropped his hand to the belt, pulling on the leather just slightly to free it from the crosspiece.

David swallowed, his stomach quivering under Trace's unintentional touch. He bit the inside of his cheek, trying hard to reverse the swelling that was going on just millimeters from Trace's fingers.

The belt prong slipped free of the punch hole, and Trace used his other hand to push the leather strap through the buckle before slipping his fingers inside David's waistband to unbutton the placket and close his fingers on the zipper tab. The heat there was stronger, warming the backs of Trace's fingers, and Trace slowly lifted his chin. His eyes ran up David's bobbing throat, chiseled chin, and scotch-wet lips that did, really did, look soft. Trace knew without a doubt that if David were a woman, he'd be kissing him right now.

The chant *Trace is not gay. He's your friend. And not gay.* took to repeating itself over and over in David's mind as he willed himself not to move, not to sway into the strong, magnetic warmth of Trace's chest only inches away. Closing his eyes, he held his breath until this torture was over. He felt his own light blond lashes flutter against his flushed cheeks. Whether flushed from the scotch or from the arousal, he wasn't sure, but they sure felt hot.

As Trace lowered the zipper, the side of his hand brushed an unmistakable bulge. The corner of his mouth quirked the tiniest bit. David was aroused too. To Trace, it looked like David was waiting. Waiting with his eyes closed... for a kiss? Heart pounding, Trace gave in to the curiosity. He tipped his head to the side and ever so slightly brushed his lips against David's.

David was sure that he imagined Trace's lips brushing ever-so-slightly against his own, warm and dry, with just a hint of scruff too. As quickly as the unexpected touch appeared, it vanished, leaving him wondering if it had ever really existed at all. Maybe his lust-soaked brain had conjured the feeling. Confused, his first impulse was to run—run and pretend that Trace was not aware of how excruciatingly turned-on he was at the moment. Of course, there was no way that Trace could mistake the ridge his knuckles had brushed. That light touch had just about made David come, and his knees were still feeling watery.

He suddenly realized that he'd been living in an almost constant state of partial arousal ever since Trace had moved in. Feeling stupid standing there with his pants open and eyes shut, swaying slightly, he forced himself to drag open his eyes to meet Trace's. "Um," he choked out, feeling his cheeks burn. *Did you just kiss me?* But his lips were frozen. Grabbing his belt to keep his pants from falling to his ankles, he turned and fled for the bathroom.

Trace watched him go, not sure at all what to say, only knowing that David's reaction had flicked something on inside him, like a light switch, and he was swamped with so much desire it embarrassed him. Once the bathroom door shut, Trace staggered to the bed, holding his head in one hand, unable to keep his other from groping himself. He was hot and hard and he just didn't know what to do about it. God, what a night. He must be losing his mind. All the innuendo and flirting and talk had certainly gone to his head, hadn't it? Why else would he be attracted to David all of a sudden? Trace looked up at himself in the mirror. *It had to be the scotch. And the circumstances.* But the feel of David's lips—they had been soft and warm. Not at all what he'd expected.

Frustrated both physically and mentally, Trace pushed himself up from the bed after a long minute and left the house, still barefoot and half-undressed, to dig in the glove compartment of his car and come up with rarely smoked cigarettes and a lighter. He walked back to the stoop and sat on the steps, lighting up with slightly shaking hands, wryly wondering what David would say. Christ. What kind of man was he? Teasing David like that. Trace hoped David wouldn't hold his actions against him.

Hiding in the bathroom, leaning back against the closed door, David's body quivered as he tried to pull himself together. What in hell was he doing? Trace was his best friend. It was a friendship that had gotten even deeper over the past week. He wasn't about to let a sudden attraction and his uncooperative body ruin that.

Gripping the edge of the sink, he ran some cold water, splashing it over his face and neck. Wiping at the droplets running down his chest with a towel, he sighed, remembering the light brush of Trace's fingers. Wetting the entire towel, he scrubbed at his skin with the cold terry cloth until his chest was red. Cursing, he tossed the towel into the hamper, stripped off his fancy suit and dropped it in a careless heap on the floor. The elastic-topped pajama bottoms he'd left on a hook behind the door were manageable, at least.

Praying that Trace had decided to crash and was already asleep, David turned off the light and cracked open the door. Expecting a dark room, he immediately tensed when he saw the light still on. But the room was empty. Had Trace left? Forgetting his embarrassment in a moment of panic, he raced through the house looking for him. Not in the office. Not in the living room. Not in the kitchen; the back door was still deadlocked. He thumped through the house and threw open the front door to check if Trace's car was gone, and he practically tripped over the man he was searching for.

Trace barely caught himself from pitching down the steps by grabbing the wrought-iron handrail. "Hey, I'm here," he said, looking up at David in surprise.

Panic subsiding as he realized Trace hadn't fled, David felt awkward, standing half-naked on his front steps. "Oh, um, sorry." He seemed to be apologizing to Trace a lot lately. "I just…. Well, you weren't…. I'd better just say good night," he finally managed to stammer out. Silently calling himself twelve kinds of fool, he turned and walked back inside. Maybe he could manage to fall asleep before Trace came back inside.

Frowning, Trace took a last drag to finish the cigarette, feeling like he had a better handle on himself. He sighed and stood up, hoping tomorrow everything went back to normal. As exciting as all this was, he wanted his friend David back. He walked back to the bedroom to see David setting an empty glass down on the dresser.

David's eyes connected with Trace's as he entered the room. Mumbling a quick, "Night," David switched off the bedside lamp and crawled into bed, arranging himself carefully on his good shoulder. Trace stood there looking at him through the dark for a minute, and then he took his turn in the bathroom, came out, and climbed into bed.

David, too wired to sleep, could tell when Trace dropped off within a few minutes, albeit somewhat restlessly. Within fifteen minutes, he had rolled to his side and unconsciously scooted across the bed to lie very close to David's back. Trace's arm was between them, curled toward himself, his knuckles brushing David's shoulder.

Still trying to fall asleep, David could feel Trace's hand against his bare skin like it was a hot brand scoring his skin. He attempted to shift away, but every time he moved, Trace followed, more and more of their bodies coming into contact. Finally, he rolled toward the other man, reaching out to touch his cheek, giving in to his desire for just a moment before he woke him to move him back to his side of the bed. But instead of waking, Trace relaxed, some of the restlessness leaving him, and he seemed to fall into a calmer sleep. Brushing a long lock of dark hair back from Trace's face, David changed his mind about waking him. His own eyelids feeling heavy, he rolled the rest of the way onto his back and let sleep claim him.

As TRACE slept, he dreamed. Dreamed of being held, of soft and lingering kisses. He could feel strong hands on his skin, hands with strength he enjoyed. Lips on his neck, his most sensitive spot, making him gasp, and the feel of a rock-hard body shifting against his, rolling on the bed, holding him, just being close.

There were occasional sparks, but for the most part he was content to lie in the strong arms wrapped around him, stealing a kiss now and then as they murmured about something he couldn't remember.

When he started to wake, Trace shifted his legs first, the warmth of the dream naturally translating to a morning erection. He vaguely remembered sleepily cuddling against a warm body because he'd been cold and the person—the man, it had to be a man—radiated heat. Now, in his fading dream, they were wrapped around each other, Trace's leg now resting securely between firm thighs. He moaned softly as he shifted, feeling a long, hot, hard brand against his own leg, and he mindlessly pushed closer, seeking some sort of stimulation for himself to help ease the buzzing in his groin. Then a strong hand moved down Trace's back to grip his hip and stop the subtle grinding, and Trace hummed quietly and stilled again, but not before burrowing closer into the warm arms wrapped around him.

He finally roused when the arms around him moved and dislodged his own hold on the warm body serving as his pillow.

David stirred as the man in his arms shifted. When he'd returned to bed the night before, he'd lain on his back and Trace had immediately cuddled against his side. Trace's leg was now resting securely between David's thighs. He groaned as the brunet moved again, his leg pressing directly against David's erection. David's hand moved down Trace's back to grip his hip and stop the subtle grinding that was going to drive him out of his mind. Trace hummed quietly and stilled again, but not before burrowing closer into the warm arms wrapped around him.

Shit. Now what? David didn't want to disturb Trace, but the man was liable to sleep another couple of hours. He attempted to slide out of Trace's arms, but Trace frowned and struggled to wake up enough to see what was wrong. "David?" he asked, his voice husky.

He knew it was David now. Had it been David just then? Trace couldn't put it together. He was too bleary. Then the shadow above him leaned forward and brushed soft lips over Trace's mouth. It was as if Trace had never left his dream. The butterfly kiss was gone so quickly Trace tried to gain another, lifting a hand to curl about the back of David's neck.

David groaned, tilting his head and deepening the kiss, their lower bodies surging forward without conscious direction. David's hand stroked down Trace's back, cupping his ass and hitching him even closer before he realized what he was doing.

Then David jerked away, leaving his skin exposed to air and chilled. He rolled out of the bed and to his feet. Without even looking at Trace, he ran a shaky hand through his sleep-mussed hair. "I'm sorry," he said, eyes darting to the man lying on his bed and then away in a blink. "I'm going… um… coffee." With one more swipe through his hair, he fled.

The warmth and pleasure investing Trace's body faltered, and he dragged his eyes open as he heard David saying something, but before he could ask him to repeat it, David was gone.

And Trace felt like he was buzzing all over.

Humming faintly, he shifted to his back, one hand straying below his hips, and he rubbed his palm over himself, hard in his boxer briefs, rocking slightly as he sank back into the dream.

ONCE David was awake, he wanted to get up and fix coffee. He took a careful sip of his second cup while staring blindly at the newspaper. He just wasn't any good at lying in bed. He certainly wasn't any good at lying in bed with Trace wrapped around him. Not that *and* keeping his hands off him. With a sigh, David rustled the paper. He shouldn't have kissed him. Not that Trace would mind, probably. But it only fed his own wants, which were destined to be unfulfilled.

Trace probably *would* mind if he'd come awake with David tilting their mouths together and deepening the kiss, their lower bodies surging forward without conscious direction, David's hand stroking down his back, cupping his ass, and hitching him even closer....

David jerked himself out of his reverie when he heard Trace banging around in the bathroom. David groaned. "Coffee. More coffee." *Is it too early to add some whiskey to it?* With a swipe of his hand through his hair, he forced himself out of the chair and over to the counter to refill his mug.

By the time he was back to his chair and had picked up the newspaper, Trace dragged into the kitchen.

"I need coffee," Trace muttered. God, he hated mornings.

"It's hot," David said, gesturing to the pot.

Trace yawned as he pulled a cup out of the cabinet. As he poured his coffee, David watched as, even half-asleep, Trace cleaned up after them before he sat down. David just had to smile.

"I'm busy today," Trace said through his yawns.

"I'm hosting the Queen for tea," David said casually.

"I have meetings from ten to four, and then I—wait. Did you just say the *Queen?*" When David laughed, Trace kicked him under the table. "It's too early to fuck around with me," he complained.

David bit his lip. "But it's fun!"

Trace threw a wadded-up napkin at him, feeling somewhat peevish now. "You're on your own for lunch. And now, I'm not sorry about it," he said pointedly. "I'll be back for an early dinner, but I've got to go back out and pick up some dry cleaning. I'm checking on Mabel on the way to the office this morning."

"What time is early?" David asked.

"Probably around five," Trace said, yawning again. "I wouldn't be up this early if Mabel wasn't being so pissy lately. She doesn't like being left alone. I'll have more shreds than curtains when I get there, I know it. But it's better than losing another pair of dress pants."

David grinned. "I wondered why that last suit came back from the cleaners without pants."

Trace rolled his eyes. "You know how hard it's going to be to find pants to match that suit now?"

"Give it up. The suit coat will look fine with khakis. You'll never match the navys," David advised.

"Thanks for the fashion advice," Trace said wryly as he stood up to take his mug to the sink. Like David knew much of anything about fashion. "You who thinks formal wear is no holes in his jeans."

"Not true! Holes in the knees are fine for formal occasions when properly paired with a nice jacket, just not holes in the ass," David responded, unable to keep the grin inside. "Unless, of course, the jacket is long enough to hide them."

Trace paused and just stared at him blankly for a long moment, and then he shook his head. "I have no reply to that." He picked up his jacket to pull it on.

David watched as Trace's jacket settled on his shoulders, his eyes naturally following the motion down as it unfortunately covered a very nice ass. *A fine-tailored suit on a fine-looking man is a wonderful thing.*

Trace picked up his laptop bag and keys and opened the door before pausing on the threshold. "Hey, you'll be okay for lunch, right?"

"Yes, Mom. I've been feeding myself for almost forty-two years."

Trace shot him a grin and stepped outside, pulling the door shut behind him.

• Chapter 7

DAVID glanced up as the doorknob rattled. After just a moment, the door opened with a thump and Matt appeared, the top of a heavy-looking, greasy bag from Five Guys Burgers and Fries clenched between his teeth. He tossed his keys on the counter and dropped the mail next to them.

"Hey, you lazy fucker, get in here. I've got your burgers."

David chuckled. "I'm right here."

Matt turned around to see David sitting with his laptop at the small kitchen table. "Enjoying your vacation?" Matt said sarcastically.

"Oh yeah, big time," David retorted, reaching out and gesturing with his good hand. "Food."

"Demanding asshole, aren't you? What, you're not still full from the other night?" Matt said as he set the bag on the table with a thump.

"Lord, don't remind me. I ate so much…."

"You telling me you didn't save room for dessert?" Matt asked with a leer as he slid a burger across the table to David.

"I saw your dessert. Chocolate éclair with cream filling was is?" David threw back.

Matt tossed a fry at David's head and said, "We're not here to talk about my love life, we're here to discuss yours."

"That's not why I asked you here," David said with a shrug before taking a bite of his burger.

"Uh huh. So why *did* you ask me over? You've been working through lunch ever since I met you. I knew there was something else," Matt said as he sat down across from him.

David sighed. "I need a favor."

"Oh Lord, here we go," Matt groaned, covering his eyes. "The last favor I did for you, I woke up in a Mexican jail cell the next afternoon."

"I bailed you out," David objected, feigning a hurt look. "But no, it's not a big favor this time. I just can't drive." He gestured to his shoulder.

"So you don't want me to drive you to Tijuana," Matt checked as he munched on his fries.

"No, just downtown."

"What do you need to go downtown for?"

David studied Matt for a long moment. He knew he was going to get teased like crazy no matter what he said. "Actually, I need to go to Trace's apartment."

Matt let out a bark of a laugh. "Why?" he drew out slowly.

"A little over a week ago I got one of those shitty migraines and called Trace to pick up my meds," David said. He raised his hand when he saw Matt start to open his mouth. "Yes, I would have called you, but you were down at that big governor's to-do, two hours away."

Matt scrunched his nose. "So you called Trace, and he brought you medicine. And dinner was a thank you?"

"No, that was Trace out reviewing restaurants. I was just tagging along," David explained.

"Uh huh," Matt said slowly. "So why are we breaking into his apartment?"

"I have a key," David qualified, frowning.

Matt just stared at him, waiting. David suppressed the urge to squirm.

"I need to go pick up his cat."

Matt's lips compressed, like he was holding back a laugh. He cleared his throat. "Aren't we a little old to be stealing the other team's mascot?"

"No, asshole. Trace has been staying with me since I fell and broke my shoulder," David said, rubbing his fingers along the strap of the sling. "There's just lots of things I can't do, and he's been helping, and his cat's been at that apartment alone for over a week now except for him running in and out for twenty minutes once a day to check on her." David could practically see all the questions running through his ex-lover's mind—to others Matt might have a hell of a poker face, but after twenty years knowing him, David was probably one of the few people who could read him.

Matt took another couple of bites of his burger; David did the same as he waited for the snappy comeback.

"So we need to go to the store and get a litter box and some cat food first," Matt said mildly.

David raised his brows in surprise. "That's it? No dig?" Matt shook his head, and David wrinkled his brow as he thought about what he might need. "I'm sure the cat has all that stuff there. We can just pick it up."

"You're not putting that litter box in my Mustang, and I'm sure as hell not cleaning that box first."

DAVID carefully pushed the door open and peeked into the apartment, fearing the cat might try to make a run for it. But no, not a feline in sight. He walked in, looking around, and Matt spoke up from behind him after he heard the door shut solidly.

"Are you sure Trace isn't secretly gay?"

David laughed. "What makes you ask that?"

"Look at this apartment! It's swank and really far too neat for any man. And the way he dresses is all sharp and neat all the time, and he owns a fucking *cat*—"

David shook his head and cut Matt off. "No, Trace is not secretly gay. There are a lot of women who would attest to that. Loudly and at length."

"I don't know, man," Matt said as he wandered over to the entertainment center. He picked up a CD. "Come on! Coldplay?" He dropped it and snatched up a DVD. "He's got *When Harry Met Sally!*"

"Hey," David objected. "I like *When Harry Met Sally!*"

"My point!" Matt announced meaningfully.

"Will you quit it? We've got to find Mabel."

"*May—bel?*"

"Hey, I didn't name her. And keep your voice down, we're probably scaring her."

David wandered back to the sunlit bedroom just in time to see a flash of fluffy black tail disappear underneath the bed with a soft jingle. He turned to call for Matt and stopped, because Matt was opening drawers in Trace's dresser. "What are you doing?" he exclaimed.

Matt turned around, a pair of black silk boxers hanging from the tip of his finger. "See? Gay."

"I'm sure those are as appealing to women as they are to men," David said drolly. *Because, oh Lord, just the thought is nearly enough to make me dizzy.*

"Have you ever known a straight man who wore silk boxers?" Matt asked, swinging the fabric back and forth.

"I've never been in a straight man's pants," David retorted, stalking over to grab the boxers and stuff them back into the dresser.

"Well, you've been in his drawers now," Matt murmured.

David smacked him in the belly with his good hand. "Mabel is under the bed."

"Ooo! The bed," Matt said spritely as he turned and made a beeline for the nightstand.

"Oh, hell no." David caught Matt's hand just in time. "Some things we just don't need to know, and a straight man's sexual habits are among them."

Matt was about to reply when Mabel streaked between them, heading out of the bedroom and into the living room. The movement surprised them both, and as they turned they bumped into one another and fell down onto the bed.

"Hey, get her!" David said as he flailed, trying to keep from rolling onto his bad shoulder.

"I've been asked to get many things in my life, but pussy isn't one of them," Matt said as he scrambled up, already in pursuit.

By the time David caught up to him out in the main room, Matt was turning toward him, his arms full of black fluff. The look on his face was one of resigned patience, and David had to laugh.

"Before you say a word," David started, "Trace got her a year ago from his grandmother when she moved to Florida," he said helplessly.

"Uh huh," Matt answered flatly. Mabel was a black Persian with long, silky, fluffy black hair, round head, flat face, and eerie orange-gold eyes. There was a collar under all that hair somewhere, but it had to be black, because all David could see was the shiny little tag and bell that had been jingling.

"Look," Matt said with a shit-eating grin, pointing to a picture on the bookshelf of Trace accepting last year's city philanthropy award, dressed in a sharp suit with his hair down and scattered over his shoulders. "They match!"

"OKAY, Mabel, the litter box is in the hall bathroom. Here's your water bowl. Here's your food." David looked down at the matching pink bowls with little kitty paw prints around the edge. "Is that enough food?"

Mabel looked up at him and blinked slowly, the tip of her tail twitching.

"I probably shouldn't be waiting for you to answer me. I think the pain meds are getting to me. Trace will be home soon. He'll fix it if it isn't right."

Mabel took two dainty steps toward the food bowl, sniffed the contents, and returned her orangey gaze to him.

"I bought seafood delight. Every cat likes fish, right?" David sighed and ran a hand through his already-mussed hair. "Damn, I'm talking to a cat. Time to go do something manly, like watching baseball." David headed for the living room. Flipping on the TV, he settled on the couch, pulling a pillow behind his head and stretching out.

"Ooof!" The air was forced from his lungs as Mabel jumped up and landed square on his gut. "Damn, you're heavier than you look."

Mabel extended her claws and began to knead at David's belly.

"Ouch! Fuck, stop that! That hurts! That's what I get for making a comment about a woman's weight." He tried to gently remove her claws from his shirt but only succeeded in repositioning her to his chest.

Turning three slow circles, Mabel settled with a throaty purr. David sighed and turned his attention to the TV, but the soothing vibrations soon lulled him to sleep.

It wasn't too much later when Trace walked in the back door and slung his laptop case onto the table next to David's computer and three used coffee mugs. He sighed and shrugged out of his jacket, hung it neatly over the back of a chair, and picked up the mugs. He rinsed them out and left them in the strainer. "David?"

When he didn't hear an answer he went looking. "Hey, David, where…."

Trace stopped in place, blinking in surprise. David was sprawled on the couch, snoring quietly, with a big, black… lump on his chest. Trace tipped his head to one side as he stepped closer.

"Mabel?" he asked in shock. Mabel raised her head from where she was curled up on top of David's slowly rising and falling chest. "What are you doing here, sweetie?" Trace asked as he walked over and hefted Mabel into his arms. Mabel mewed in protest and tried to squirm as he held onto her. Trace kept her close and nudged David's side with his knee. "Hey, David. David."

Finally David's eyes fluttered open. He saw Trace, but it didn't register at first. Rubbing his eyes, David sat up carefully. "Hi," he said with a yawn.

"Hi," Trace said, amused. "Is there a reason you're sleeping with my cat? I thought you weren't into women?"

David added, "Or cats," in a mutter. "And let me tell you, she sure is a woman."

"What do you mean?" Trace asked as he sat down on the other end of the couch, stroking Mabel the way he knew she liked, but she kept squirming. He frowned down at her.

"I stupidly commented on her weight, and she clawed the hell out of me," David groused, rubbing his chest as he watched Trace fumbling to keep hold of the cat.

"And again I ask, what is she doing here?" Trace asked, really confused. Mabel hissed and bit down on Trace's finger, and he reflexively let go with a yelp. Mabel climbed off him with a sniff and slinked right over to David's lap, where she settled down with a happy purr. David looked down at her, bemused, and then up at Trace, who laughed. "Looks like you have a girlfriend," he managed to get out between snorts.

"I guess there's a first time for everything," David said, sliding his fingers along her head. Mabel purred louder and rubbed against his palm.

"She likes you better than me!" Trace complained. "I've been trying to get her to love me for months!"

David just cleared his throat and looked around innocently. "I rescued the damsel in distress from near starvation and touch deprivation in an isolated castle," he claimed.

Trace rolled his eyes. "Fine," he muttered. He sighed and figured it was for the best. Mabel had thrown two temper tantrums in just the past three days, one of which had resulted in a destroyed pair of suit pants. "She'll be happier here anyway."

David gave him an apologetic look. "Since you're here, there's no reason she shouldn't be. I hated the thought of her being alone in that apartment. I mean, with all you're doing for me—"

"I'm doing it because I want to, David, not because I want something back." Trace stopped and had to smile. It was really kind of sweet. "Thanks. It's really nice to have her here." He squinted at David. "Even if she does like you better."

David shrugged, and a thought occurred to him that made him grin. "Who'd have thought I'd ever have a chance to steal a woman from you?"

Trace's lips twitched. "Don't spoil her too much. She'll be hell when I have to take her back home. Although she didn't really see me all that much more before I've been here," he had to admit.

"Yeah, your apartment looks barely lived in," David agreed, thinking about the overly neat rooms.

"Hey, how'd you get there?" Trace felt a flash of alarm. "You didn't drive, did you?" He thought about the bottle of narcotics in the bathroom he'd been carefully dosing David with.

"No, no. I called Matt to come and pick me up," David assured him.

"Matt. The photographer," Trace recalled.

"Yeah. He was glad to help," David said. "He had all sorts of compliments about your apartment." Not that he'd be sharing them with Trace. "Mabel liked him too."

Trace sighed. "I'm starting to think Mabel might be a fag hag," he muttered.

David hugged her close protectively. "Hey! That's my girl you're dissing."

Mabel looked at Trace from David's arms, and Trace could have sworn she stuck her tongue out at him. *Damn cat.* He decided he didn't want to consider too closely why he felt a streak of jealousy shoot through him.

• Chapter 8

TRACE shifted for the twelfth time in the hard plastic chair and sighed as he flipped through the *Entertainment Weekly* he'd nabbed off the magazine rack. There was no point in reading the local *GO!* lifestyle and entertainment magazine sitting on the low table in front of him—he'd written more than half of it.

He glanced up when the door that led back into the treatment areas opened, but a grandma-type lady with her walker tromped out instead of David. Wrinkling his nose, Trace turned another page. David must have been doing okay with the physical therapy, because he'd been back there for the full hour this time. This was his second visit, and Trace wasn't sure he was looking forward to the end of it. After the first appointment last week, David had been a real bear. He'd have thought David broke his arm yesterday, not almost three weeks ago.

The door swung open again with less force than the grandma had generated, and David shuffled through, his good shoulder curved forward as he cradled his right arm. His eyes darted up long enough to locate Trace before returning to the floor as he walked across the room. Rubbing his forearm through the sling, he offered a weak smile. "They added two new exercises this week. I swear the healing hurts more than the breaking."

Trace tried not to wince as he saw how tired David looked. "How about some lunch and then pain relief?" he suggested.

David grimaced and swallowed a wave of nausea brought on by the echoing pain lapping through his chest. "I think maybe we need to reverse that."

"Not if you want to keep the pills down," Trace said mildly as he stood and started herding David toward the door. "We'll try something like crackers first, just until you can take the medicine, then more substantial food. You don't want to be ill all night like last time." And hadn't that been about the limit Trace wanted to deal with for *anyone*.

"Before Beelzebub in there got his hands on me, I was going to suggest seafood at that little place on the pier. Now all I want to do is crawl into bed and drug myself into oblivion. How can something that is supposed to be good for me hurt so fuckin' much?"

A woman seated by the door to the office looked up and snorted at the language. Trace glanced over, and they exchanged wry smiles. "We'll compromise. Crackers, drugs, nap, then dinner on the pier," Trace said soothingly as he opened the front door and gestured for David to go ahead.

"Can I take my pills with scotch?"

"Move," Trace said with a bit more authority, waving his hands toward the car and ignoring David's crack. Having an argument when David was hurting was not a good idea, and Trace had no plans to start one. "Sooner home, sooner drugs."

David collapsed in the car seat, his head tilted back, eyes closed. He quit guarding his hurt arm just long enough to fasten his seatbelt. "If you were a good mom you'd have crackers in your pocket... or purse... or wherever they keep them to pull out and shove into their baby's mouth at restaurant tables. I've never quite understood that. They have crackers... even when they don't serve crackers at the restaurant...." David continued to ramble, hissing as the car passed over the speed bumps on the way out of the parking lot. He knew he was being seriously cranky, but he just couldn't summon the energy to be positive right now.

Trace bit his lip as David drawled on brokenly about whatever caught his attention. He could only hope that David would stay more detached and less annoyed. "My parenting skills are sorely lacking, I'm afraid, as Mabel is well aware."

"You're better than you think," David mumbled, staring out at the traffic on his side of the car.

Raising an eyebrow, Trace smiled a little. "Thanks."

David shrugged with one shoulder and waved his hand in dismissal. He didn't want Trace to see that he was more than a little embarrassed. After a few quiet minutes, he spoke up. "I hate to even mention it, but I'm afraid if I don't I'll chicken out." David shifted in the seat, obviously not able to find a comfortable position. "Dr. Mengele wants me to do a series of extensions and rotations three times a day, but I've got to have someone help me support the arm's weight as I do them. I know the last thing you need is something else I need help with—"

"David, it's no problem. I want to help," Trace said, trying not to let any frustration leak out into his voice. He'd told David that time and time again, but it seemed like his best friend was sure he was going to just run out on him. "It'll be fine. Breakfast, lunch, and dinner," he pointed out as he navigated through traffic. "I'm already home for those most of the time."

"I'm torn between being grateful and wishing you'd say 'Hell no!' so I could go back next week and tell them I couldn't find anyone to help. I'd call Matt, but a nurse he's not…"

Trace looked at David sideways as the man kept rambling. He was acting like he was already drugged up. Exhaustion?

"… still, he might be able to help with the midday one if you are working. Not exactly sure what Matt does with his days, but I'm pretty certain, it doesn't involve work." David chuckled, his eyes starting to drift closed again.

Trace sighed and took a look at David as he brought the car to a halt at a stoplight, and he raised his hand before he realized it, reaching over to brush David's hair out of his eyes. Seemed like it was just long enough to get messy like that every time they were in the convertible with the top down. David screwed up his face, and Trace yanked his hand back. "How does Matt do that?" David complained, and Trace relaxed as he was off and rattling off whatever. Trace suspected it was a way to keep his mind off the pain. With a last smile, Trace got the car moving again.

"ARE you sure you really want to do this?" David had been grumbling and complaining ever since Trace walked into the kitchen a full forty-five minutes earlier than usual the next morning. He frowned even more when Trace blithely ignored him in favor of the coffeepot and English muffin.

"I mean, really," David continued, "you don't want to start your day off dealing with grouchy me in pain, do you?"

Trace continued to deliberately tune him out as he popped his breakfast into the toaster and went to the fridge to pull out butter and jelly.

David nervously rubbed at his forearm where it lay comfortably in the sling below a right-now-not-hurting shoulder. He really would prefer it to stay not-hurting. "I'm sure I'll be able to handle it on my own, at least these first few times, you know, until I'm a little more recovered from my torture session yesterday."

When Trace finally turned around with his coffee cup and leaned back against the counter, David sighed. He could clearly read the "Bullshit" comment on Trace's face. "Damn," David muttered. Trace's lips twitched as he snagged his muffin out of the toaster and set it on the table next to the condiments. "Slave driver," David added petulantly.

Trace snorted. "Big baby," he said as he yawned and spread grape jelly. "Ten minutes and it'll be all over." And maybe he'd see how not-bad it was and calm down about it all.

"Until lunch time," David retorted.

"Then ten minutes and it'll be all over."

David sniffed and picked up his coffee. He wasn't sure what was up with Trace this morning; usually he was a lot more... asleep.

"Until dinner."

Trace actually smiled, marveling a little at the humor of David's overreaction. "Cranky this morning?" he asked politely.

"I don't want to hurt again," David admitted.

Trace shrugged. "Hurt now and get better. Don't hurt now, don't get better, hurt later," he said through a mouthful of muffin.

David squinted at him. "You are far too laid-back about all this."

"Would you rather me be a hard-ass?" Trace asked reasonably.

"It's hard to get mad at you when you're this calm and helpful."

"Part of my master plan," Trace admitted as he polished off half the muffin. "Did you eat?"

"Yes, *Mom*," David sniped. He knew he was being childish and that it looked really bad on a forty-two-year-old man. But not only was he not looking forward to the exercises, he was operating on a night of crappy sleep. He'd thought several times about how Trace's hands would feel on him, gently supporting his arm, brushing against his wrist.... David shook himself. Trace was staring at him. Had he been talking to him? "What?"

"I said, do you want to do the exercises here where you can sit in the kitchen chair, or in the living room so you can slump on the couch after?"

"Oh, living room, definitely. Closer to the scotch too," David muttered as he stood and walked in that direction, ignoring the small smile he'd seen on Trace's face.

He collapsed on the couch, telling himself to grow up. Being a big baby would just annoy Trace, who'd leave, and where would that leave him and his barely healed shoulder? He rubbed at his eyes and told himself he needed to suck it up.

"Sling off, please," Trace said as he walked in with the piece of paper the therapist have given David to take home. Taking a deep breath and steeling himself, he slid on his glasses on and started studying the diagrams. "This shouldn't be too bad."

"You're not the one with the broken shoulder."

Trace didn't respond to the jibe as he sat down next to David "All right. First exercise. You're going to hold your arm, elbow bent at ninety degrees, and lift it up and out, away from your body."

David watched as Trace copied the movement drawn on the sheet, and he had to stifle a laugh.

"What?" Trace glanced up at him.

"You look like a chicken," David snickered.

"Well, I am the cock of the roost. C'mon, chickadee. Flap that wing," Trace instructed with a wink.

David sighed and slowly lifted his arm, afraid of the shooting pains he'd suffered at physical therapy yesterday. Luckily, his shoulder just felt very stiff and sore.

"Lift it a little further," Trace said as he took hold of David's elbow gently to help. He was perched on the edge of the couch, and their knees bumped. "Your elbow needs to stop on an even line with your shoulder."

David almost shivered as he felt tingles where Trace touched him. But a minute later he was frowning as his arm started feeling heavy. "No wonder I need help."

"Why is that?"

"My arm already feels like it weighs a hundred pounds."

Little furrows appeared between Trace's brows, and he told himself not to worry. David was a big boy; he could handle it. "Okay, ten times is enough."

David sighed and let his arm hang, which actually hurt a little too. He was used to having it supported. "What's next, coach?"

"Holding your arm in the same position to start, this time pull your fist straight up over your shoulder so your forearm is parallel with the ceiling and then back down again."

Another snicker. "You look like Tiger Woods."

Trace rolled his eyes. "Five times."

By the time David had finished those and two more exercises, he was gritting his teeth. "Is that all?" he ground out. He glanced up to see Trace watching him, but he couldn't tell what Trace was thinking. "Is it?"

"Ah, yes," Trace said, setting the paper on the table, quietly proud that David hadn't quit.

"Finally," David huffed, scooting sideways and reaching for his sling.

"Why don't you go ahead and take a shower before putting that back on?" Trace suggested.

"Maybe I don't want to take a shower," David snapped, ignoring the light sweat along his hairline and between his shoulder blades. He felt so weak, for such stupid, tiny exercises to wear him out so quickly. He stood up without warning and pushed past Trace's knees, not caring that he about knocked his best friend back into the couch. He stomped back to the bedroom and stood in front of the mirror, sulking.

With a sigh he sat on the edge of the bed and set his forehead in his hand. He was being such an asshole about this. There was no reason to be mean to Trace, who was going so out of his way to help.

David felt something move against his calves, and he looked down to see Mabel weaving around his ankles. She stopped and purred as she rubbed against his leg. Shaking his head, he reached down to rub between her ears. When he looked up into the mirror, he saw Trace standing quietly in the doorway behind him, sling in hand.

"I'm sorry, Trace," David said with heartfelt resignation. "I'm being a bastard, and you don't deserve it."

Trace didn't say anything right away as he lingered in the doorway. There really wasn't anything to say. So he held out the sling. David stood up and walked over to take it with a murmured thank you.

"I'll be back at lunch. Subway okay?" Trace asked, hoping that just moving on with the day would help David shed some of the crankiness. He reached out to pat David's chest supportively.

David nodded, and he blinked at him when he felt a gentle warmth on his chest. He looked down to see Trace's hand there, just touching as he looked at his best friend. It was... soothing. Reassuring. And he knew that Trace understood. "You know what I like," David said softly.

Trace smiled, and David was struck by how true what he'd just said was.

TRACE yawned as he brushed his hair back, his other hand gathering it at his nape so he could tie it back. He wasn't quite used to the whole get-up-early thing yet—well, early for him, anyway. For a society night owl, even an hour earlier, for such a good cause as helping David with his PT, was still quite an adjustment.

He blinked his eyes hard several times as he tossed the brush into the basket on the vanity and grabbed a washcloth. As the water warmed up, he studied his own face in the mirror, idly wondering what David saw when he looked at him. Sighing, Trace sniffed and stuck the cloth under the water.

Since that night in the car, his mind kept edging back toward that vision of David in the seat next to him, face soft and relaxed as he dozed, and how silky David's hair had felt between his fingers. How he'd felt *something* sitting there in the dark next to David.

Letting out a rough exhale, Trace turned off the tap and held the cloth over his cheeks to warm the skin so he could shave. He swallowed and shut his eyes as he leaned his hip against the vanity, feeling his cheeks warm… and it wasn't only from the washcloth. It was too easy to remember how that jolt of arousal had shocked him—

—and how it still did. He opened his eyes and recognized that same yank of desire pulling at him as his cock swelled. Trace groaned. *This has to stop.* A straight man does not lust after his gay friend.

Does he?

Staring at himself, he tried to evaluate how he felt about it. Could he, a longtime ladies' man—because he did love the ladies and everything about them—really be attracted to another man? His stomach flip-flopped. Frowning, Trace tried to pinpoint what really bothered him about it by how his gut reacted. Was he worried about what other people would think? *No, I don't think so. I've pretty much always done my own thing anyway. And I've got a few other friends who are gay, so it's not like I'm not familiar with the concept.* Upset? *No. How could I be upset at David? It's not his fault I'm having a minor identity crisis.* Freaked out? *A little.* He blinked. *Okay, more than a little, but maybe crisis is too strong a word.* Angry? *No, not at all. More like... confused. Why is this happening* now? Turned on? *...Oh hell.*

Trace grimaced, dropped the washcloth, and picked up the can of shaving gel to get started shaving as his brain continued to pick apart his problem. Why turned on? *Because he looked... incredible in that suit. And handsome. Very handsome.* Why is that affecting you now? *I don't know. Proximity? Our friendship is getting closer? He's my best friend?* Be honest. *Fuck. He... turns me on. And I have no clue what to do about it.*

Tossing the razor in the sink a couple of minutes later, Trace met his own eyes in the mirror. Does it really change things? *Yes.* For the worse? *No.* Are you sure? *Very sure.* For the better? *I know David will be my friend no matter what. Maybe, just maybe, he could be something more?*

Chewing on that idea, Trace went to get dressed, coming to some sort of peace with it, if not with the execution of it.

I'll just have to wait and see. Maybe I'll feel differently later.

Feeling much more stable, Trace shrugged off the uncertainty and went to join David in the kitchen. "Coffffffeeeeee," he moaned, holding his arms out and walking stiffly like a zombie.

"Fucker." David swatted at him playfully as he passed, and Trace shuffled along, grinning and shifting his hips in an unsuccessful effort to miss David's swipe. "You already abused my scotch. You better savor my coffee, or I'll be sending you out to McDonald's."

Trace noticed his favorite sections of the newspapers were folded next to his plate. David had also toasted two bagels, and the cream cheese was on the table waiting for Trace to spread it on both of them. Spreading cream cheese was one of the things they'd discovered was almost impossible to do one-handed.

"Well, McDonald's coffee isn't quite so bad since they went to the new stuff. But if you want really, really good coffee? You go to Waffle House." Trace mmmm-mmmmm-ed to reinforce his point as he pried open the small tub of cream cheese and started spreading it. A lot on his bagel, a little on David's.

"Heathen!" David accused. "How dare you compare my fresh-ground French roast to Waffle House slop?" Taking a bite of his bagel, he disappeared back behind his paper, shifting down in his chair and propping his feet on the seat of Trace's, his bare toes burrowing under Trace's thigh for warmth.

Good-naturedly shifting to allow for David's toes, Trace took a bite and shrugged, at the same time acknowledging the tiny zing he felt. "Who's the food critic, hmmm? I've had coffee all over this city. I should know," he said, thumping the newspaper next to his plate with a knuckle.

Almost two hours flew by as the two men did David's physical therapy exercises, made their way through most of an eight-cup pot of coffee, and read all three newspapers, passing sections back and forth in silence other than the occasional exclamation. Folding the last section and pulling his laptop forward, David sighed. "I guess I should get a little writing done before the guys show up. Are you gonna stick around for poker tonight?"

"Ooo, is that an official invitation?" Trace asked with a grin, pleased by the idea. It had been awhile since he'd done something really social, and he was missing it. "I'm still no good at poker, but I'll hang around awhile… if only for another chance at that scotch," he said, waggling his eyebrows. Then he smiled warmly. "I'd also like to meet your friends."

David glowered back. "I don't know. If Matt sees you guzzling his four-hundred-dollar-a-bottle scotch, he's liable to shoot you. At the very least, he won't help you escape Katherine's clutches at this year's bachelor auction. But yes, if you think you can behave, I'd like to have you come."

Trace affected a chastened look. "I'll be good, I promise!" he said earnestly, eyes sparkling, lips pursed into a smile as he tried to hold back a laugh.

"Good. Think you could make it to the grocery store this afternoon? I'm still not supposed to drive because of those damn blessed pain pills, and if we leave it to the guys to bring food, we'll be drinking dinner."

"Sure. I've got a few hours in the office and an interview at a gallery downtown this afternoon. I can go after that. What do you want me to get?" Trace asked, leaning back to sip his last cup of coffee. It struck him, out of the blue, how domestic this all seemed. It made him smile. Who'd have thought it would feel so good?

"I'll make you a list while you grab a shower. In case you hadn't noticed, it's almost ten." David laughed as Trace jumped up from the table.

"Damn it!" Trace exclaimed as he took two steps, then two steps back to put down the coffee cup, and rushed out of the kitchen.

• Chapter 9

DAVID moved around the kitchen, setting out glasses, brewing a pot of coffee, and filling the ice bucket. Trace had dashed through the door minutes ago, just barely ahead of the other guys. He was in the bedroom cleaning up.

Keeping busy to resist the urge to join him and catch a glimpse of the body that had been on his mind all day, David opened a bag of cheese cubes that had a zip closure, grateful that Trace seemed to have picked things in packages he could open, since he was still wearing the damn sling after almost a month. He didn't technically need it all the time, but tonight he didn't want to deal with an aching shoulder.

He poured the cheese into a black stoneware bowl and tossed the plastic in the trash before adding the bowl to the lineup of other food on the counter, where they'd eat buffet style when the steaks were done. Before he could pick up a jar of olives to carry out to the bar in the dining room, he heard Trace's voice from the back of the house.

"David? Have you seen my red shirt? It's not in the closet, and I'm sure I left it here."

"Yeah," David shouted back, moving toward the laundry room. "I threw it in the wash. Just a sec. I'll get it." Snatching the hanger off the rod where he'd hung the shirt out of the dryer, David walked down the hall and into the bedroom with the requested item. "Here you go."

Trace was standing with his back to the door, pulling up his well-fitted black pants over clinging boxer briefs. "Thanks," he said distractedly as he settled the pants on his hips, leaving them unfastened so he could tuck the shirt in. He turned around to reach for it.

David gulped. Trace had pulled off his tie and white dress shirt, leaving himself bare-chested as he turned around. David's eyes lingered on the muscled chest and the enticing line of dark hair traveling down from Trace's belly button to disappear beneath his underwear. Forcing his eyes back up, he watched with fascination as Trace's nipples hardened under his gaze.

Whatever this was that was happening between them definitely wasn't one-sided, and that knowledge spread warmth through David's body. He glanced up, and Trace met his gaze steadily. Taking the shirt off the hanger, David stepped forward, intending to drape it around Trace's shoulders just as the doorbell rang. Catching Trace's eyes with a regretful look, he shrugged, turning away to answer the door.

Trace went still as he saw David looking him over frankly, and a zing rippled through him. He blinked and tilted his head. So last night wasn't a fluke caused by scotch. He shifted his weight to move forward when he heard the bell, and the regret on David's face was clear. Trace wondered what David would have done. "David."

David's heart, racing from his intimate examination of Trace's chest, skipped a beat as Trace spoke his name. It sounded husky, low, and full of promise, but.... One side of David's mouth curled up in a smile. *Just ask,* he thought. *Ask me to stay, and I'll ignore the door and the people on the other side forever.* "I'd better get the door," he murmured after a long moment of mutual quiet.

Trace took two steps to stop at David's side and lifted the shirt from his hand before he could leave the room. Reassured by David's appraisal and the husk in his voice, Trace smiled slowly. He'd have never thought that discovering a man was aroused by him would feel so good. "Thanks. Go on," he said. "I'll be out in a minute."

Head still back in the bedroom with Trace, David wandered down the hall and to the kitchen to open the door for Patrick and John. He could see Jared pulling into the driveway. Matt would be late; he always was.

John's eyebrows pulled together in concern as he shrugged out of his suit jacket, looking David over and noting the sling. "You okay?" he asked.

David smiled to put his friend at ease. "Leave your doctor's bag in the car, John. I hurt my shoulder few weeks ago. It's just now healing and is still a little tender."

"Tender? You broke it," Trace commented in amusement from where he'd stopped just inside the room. David looked. Trace had finished getting dressed, including tucking the red shirt in, which with the black belt only emphasized his trim waist. But he'd left the top two buttons on his shirt undone, looking cool and stylish with his hair finger-combed behind his ears. He'd fit right in, since the other men were arriving in suits in various states of disarray after long days at work.

The glare David shot in his direction was filled with more fondness than anger. "Yes, tender. Let's go into the dining room. Guys, this is Trace. Trace, John and Patrick." Unconsciously, he stroked his hand over Trace's middle as he walked past, his fingers curling around Trace's side just above his belt before dropping back to his side.

As they moved toward the large, round black and grey marble table, Patrick pulled David to the side. "New lover?" he asked, one eyebrow raised in a peaked arch.

A chill settled around David's shoulders. He hadn't considered his nosy friends' take on his relationship with Trace. Their not-so-thoughtful teasing could ruin something as gentle and new as what was building between them. "Aw hell. No," he answered casually as he picked up a bottle of liquor to add to the bar. "You've seen my type. Trace is one of my closest friends, and he's just helping out. More than I can say for you fuckers, who never stop by or even call until it's time for poker night again."

Turning to watch the others pass, Trace bit his lip when he heard David's easy response to some too-quiet question, one he could easily figure out. It wasn't what David said to answer it that confused him or, much less, bothered him. It was the twinge of disappointment he felt upon hearing it.

Trace blinked as he recalled how his body had responded to David's focused gaze. *Wow.* He could feel the tension zipping between them—something that had been growing for a while now. And Trace knew he didn't want it to end. He'd gone still as he saw David looking him over boldly, and a flash of desire had rippled through him.

Trace blinked and tilted his head. It wasn't just a fluke of circumstance—he was feeling it again and again, and more often. He rubbed his hand over his belly where David's hand had touched him. They were still best friends, he reminded himself. *No matter what.*

With that determination, Trace picked up the ice bucket David had filled and carried it into the dining room, where a couple of the guys were finding seats, drinks already in hand, joking and laughing as Jared shuffled the cards. Trace was about to return to the kitchen to see if there were any more bottles that needed to be put out when a voice stopped him.

"Trace! What a surprise!"

Turning halfway around, Trace grinned. "Hey, Matt. Welcome to the party. I hear you trounce these yahoos regularly. I didn't know you were handy with anything but a camera."

"Oh, I have many talents. Just ask David." Matt shot David an exaggerated leer, spurring roars of laughter from the guys who were used to Matt and David's innuendo and flirting. Trace enjoyed the playful banter. This was hardly any different from a night out with some of his own friends. He could handle this.

"Including catnapping?" Trace asked.

"Catnapping?" Patrick asked.

Matt laughed as he sat down and waved Patrick off. "I was just an accessory, I promise. But I *do* have skills."

"Punctuality not being one of them. Shut up and deal," David ordered, everyone taking their seats after making drinks and loosening collars. He cocked his head, looking at Trace when he took a seat on the opposite side of the table.

"Don't deal me in. I'm just an observer," Trace said easily, accepting a tumbler of vodka twist from Matt.

"That don't fly with this group. We don't do observers. If you stay, you play," Patrick teased, patting a chair beside him. "I'll help."

With a doubtful smirk, Trace shifted over next to him. "All right, but I'm warning you. David tried to teach me the basics, and it didn't go well." He glanced up at David as he settled back down.

"I'm a much better teacher than David. Right, fellas?" Patrick said. A chorus of jeers answered his comment, and they all contributed chips to the newcomer.

As he leaned over to talk to Matt, David felt a niggling of unease as Patrick's attention focused on Trace, the physical therapist angling his chair so that their knees had to be touching. Other than Matt, Patrick was the only other member of their group that had any interest in men. He wasn't gay, but he was definitely bi, and Trace was downright gorgeous tonight.

Trace watched Matt's and David's heads close together, making him wonder. *No. Not Matt.* Trace would have noticed before. Besides, David had said they had a history. Not a "now." He shifted his attention back to Patrick, who leaned closer to him with one elbow on the table while talking about strategy. Trace was certain Patrick was flirting with him. Lips twitching, Trace listened to Patrick murmur a question about the cards. *No harm in a little flirting, after all.*

John had just called a bet and tossed in some chips when out of nowhere Mabel jumped up onto the table, scattering chips and cards everywhere. Patrick and Matt just barely managed to save their drinks from toppling over.

"Mabel!" Trace chastised as he stood up and tried to reach across the table to capture her.

"Mabel?" Jared echoed.

"Ah. Catnapping," Patrick said knowingly.

"Oh Lord, I am still scarred," Matt moaned. David threw some cards at him.

Mabel hissed and swiped, just evading Trace's hands and slinking around the table to hop down into David's lap, where she settled and started licking her paw.

Matt slowly grinned. "So. *That's* how it is."

"She likes him better," Trace complained, sitting down with a thump.

"I didn't know you had a cat," John said as he tried to straighten up the chips.

"He doesn't," Matt said at the same time as David said, "She's Trace's."

John and Jared started chuckling as Patrick said, "Doesn't look like she's Trace's anymore."

Matt snickered. "David stole himself a woman."

David smacked Matt in the chest with the back of his good hand before he went back to petting Mabel.

"At least she has good taste," Trace muttered, and Patrick, mid-swallow, about choked on his drink as he started laughing.

"All right, that hand's out," Jared pronounced as he started dealing.

Trace noticed that Mabel didn't look like she was going anywhere anytime soon, and he sighed as he recognized that little bit of jealousy turn to longing as he watched David's fingers slide through Mabel's fur.

DAVID'S discomfort, which had started when Patrick began "helping" Trace with his cards, grew over the next couple of hours of poker and a dinner break, once Jared finished grilling the steaks. Patrick's attention was clearly focused on Trace and had not wavered all night. It was really starting to get on David's nerves, and he knew that by all rights it shouldn't. But that didn't really help much.

A foot kicked David's shin, and Matt leaned close to his ear. "You need to find your poker face. You're not winning anything tonight," Matt warned. "And the guys are starting to notice."

David tossed his cards into the center of the table for the fourth hand in a row. "I fold." Poker took concentration, and all of his attention was centered on the two men flirting on the opposite side of the table. Patrick had folded earlier and was currently draped over Trace's shoulder helping him play his hand.

"Time for dessert. Come help me, David," Matt said, throwing in his cards as well, pushing out of his chair and nudging his friend.

David rolled his eyes. Matt wasn't known for his subtlety. He got to his feet anyway. If he didn't follow, there was no telling what Matt would say or do. He picked up the empty ice bucket and followed.

Once in the kitchen, Matt turned on David, his voice hushed. "Is something going on between you and Trace?" he asked flat out.

"Doesn't appear to be," David stated, opening the refrigerator and pointing at a box displaying a label from The Cheesecake Factory.

"Only if you've got your eyes shut," Matt retorted as he pulled the box out and set it on the table. "There's sparks flying off the two of you like fireworks. And Patrick is just eating it up, since you're doing your best to ignore it."

"Maybe hanging around me has opened Trace's eyes to the possibilities of attraction to men. He certainly is looking at Patrick differently than he would have a month ago." David busied himself setting out saucers one at a time, trying to be nonchalant about the conversation.

"Hanging around? Since when has Trace been hanging around, anyway? And why were you out to dinner that night? That was a pretty spiffy dinner for two 'friends,'" Matt needled. "How come you never talk about him?"

"We've been friends for a long time, and I hang out with him at different times than I do with you all." David said, knowing that sounded crazy. "I told you I hurt my shoulder, and he was already here. He's a good friend."

Matt tilted his head to one side, studying David. "I shouldn't have to say this to a Fulbright scholar, but hanging around to take care of super-grouch you for four weeks is a *little* more than just friendship. So spill. He's more than a good friend, isn't he?" he asked.

David and Matt had tried being together for a while before it became obvious they were better off as pals, and that was years ago. They were still close friends. So if anyone was going to notice David's interest in another man, it would be Matt. David braced his hip against the counter. "I thought… maybe. That night at the restaurant? That was just business. Trace was doing reviews, but

110

something was building." He looked up sheepishly. "Pretty pathetic, huh? I'm too old to be falling for straight friends."

"Or at least your straight friend's cat." Matt stepped to the counter to get some napkins and took a casual look out into the dining room at the poker table. David knew what he was seeing: Patrick was still flirting heavily, much to John and Jared's amusement. While Trace wasn't exactly encouraging it, he was obviously enjoying it. The corner of Matt's mouth quirked as he watched Trace subtly flirt back. He turned back to David, eyes dancing. "You sure he's totally straight?"

"No," David said with a groan. "Actually at this point, I'm pretty sure he's bi-curious." And David wished he knew how that had happened.

Matt's smile soon matched his eyes. "And would it be you who introduced him to the curious stage?" he drawled, wagging his eyebrows over mischievous eyes.

"Pervert," David accused, but it had no heat. His bemusement returned as he glanced out at the table, seeing Trace's forehead fall onto Patrick's shoulder as he laughed. "I don't think I did, but Trace has obviously decided to do a little exploring on his own."

"You've got it bad, haven't you?" Matt said quietly, shaking his head. He glanced back out to the poker game. "Hell. Trace is a notorious flirt; that's known all over town. He's dated most of the eligible women, and most of them would kill for another go at him." Matt placed a friendly hand on David's good shoulder as he sent ice clinking into his glass with the other. "So just think about this: He's taken care of you. He's moved in with you to do it. And I'll bet he's made a regular habit of doing up your pants. Patrick's not a threat."

David flushed at the accuracy of Matt's assessment. He'd known Matt long enough to know that he sometimes saw things that others missed. "Why isn't Patrick a threat?"

Matt's smile was back as he picked up a fresh scotch bottle. "Because in between laughing and the negligible bit of flirting Trace is doing, he's watching us. Correction. Watching *you*. Just like he has since I got here."

"I haven't felt this way about someone in a long time, but...." David looked up at his friend with a rueful smile. "I'm telling this to the wrong person, aren't I?"

Toasting David with a freshly poured glass, Matt winked and headed back out to the poker table, asking loudly what he'd missed and why the hell were some of his chips gone, leaving David to his conflicted thoughts.

Trace watched Matt come back to the table, and when David didn't immediately follow, his brow creased. Was David hiding out in the kitchen? It wouldn't take that long to set out dishes for dessert, not even one-armed. Maybe he needed some help and didn't want to admit it in front of his other friends? After another long minute, he threw in his hand despite the three of a kind and slinked out of the chair, using his mostly empty glass as an excuse to escape to the kitchen.

He didn't see Matt's grin.

"David? You okay?" Trace asked as he stepped through the doorway into the kitchen.

"Yeah, just getting the cheesecake out to sit so we can cut it without hacking it up," David said, holding up the bottle of scotch. "Refill? You're not driving."

"Please," Trace answered, looking at David quizzically as he stopped next to him at the table. David's blond hair was a little ruffled, the result of dragging his hands through it while playing his cards, and he looked very handsome in his pressed shirt with the sleeves rolled neatly and charcoal suit pants.

After watching a bit of scotch gurgle into the glass, Trace said, "Your friends are a hoot."

"Hmmm." David answered noncommittally. "I'm having a serious problem with one of them at the moment." Without warning, he swung away from the counter, trapping Trace between his body and the cabinets.

Trace's eyes widened as his ass bumped the counter and a little of the scotch in the glass sloshed over his fingers. "What kind of problem?" he asked, eyes flickering over David's face. This was totally new behavior, in Trace's experience, this slightly dominant turn—though he acknowledged he was finding it very appealing. And if he didn't know better, Trace would have thought he was being maneuvered into a torrid kiss.

"I seem to have become a little intolerant." David's fingers brushed Trace's hair back from his face. "Of *anyone* touching you." Leaning forward, he pressed their bodies together. "But *me*," he growled.

The tone of David's voice, the heat of his proximity, and the press of his contoured body had Trace shivering before he could repress it, and he couldn't tear his gaze away from David's flashing blue eyes. It registered with Trace that he was aroused again, just by those few words and the possessiveness implied. It made him reexamine his thoughts from when he'd been watching David and Matt pal around. Did he want this?

The ball of desire starting to roil in his gut answered his question. "A little intolerant?" he asked, one hand closing carefully on David's elbow, since he still had the glass of scotch in the other. *Yeah.* Yeah, he wanted it. He wanted to pull David closer to feel the heat from his skin.

"Well, I'm not sure that you even want me to touch you, so I can't be much more than that, can I?" David stroked Trace's cheek with the side of one thumb. "Do you, Trace?" he rasped. "Do you want me to touch you?"

Trace was stunned. He was being seduced. Skillfully seduced. And he was *loving* it. Riveted by the magnetism pouring off David and the contrast of his soft touch, Trace slid one hand to David's good shoulder, tipped his head to the side, and *what the hell, why not?* slowly lifted his mouth to press their lips together. He wanted to know what it felt like, that passion burning in David's eyes. David moaned, tilting his head to fit their mouths together more firmly. His free hand slid down Trace's side, fingers clutching at his hip.

"David, it's your deal!" Matt yelled from the other room, his voice heavily laced with amusement. David and Trace pulled apart abruptly, turning their chins to look toward the doorway that had just enough angle to shield them from view.

Trace turned heated eyes back to David. "I do," he said huskily before giving David a rakish smile. He sauntered back to the dining room, doing his best to hide the little bit of trembling in his hands and the large chunk of thundering in his pulse. He was more turned on than he would have believed possible from kissing a man. No, not just a man, he was almost sure it was from kissing *David*.

Trace retook his seat, setting his glass at his elbow, and inhaled long and slow, trying to settle his breathing as he listened to the game and the banter going on around him. He'd almost succeeded when David walked back into the dining room and to the table to lean over Trace's shoulder. David slid his fingers into the long dark hair that fell over Trace's shoulder and pulled it back from his neck as he lowered his lips to Trace's ear.

"I'd probably be a bad host if I kicked everyone out, huh?" David whispered conspiratorially, running his lips down Trace's exposed neck until Trace shivered in reaction as the unexpected heat and arousal bloomed again.

David was leaving no doubt with anyone in the room about how he felt about his houseguest.

Trace's eyes fluttered shut for a few seconds as he fought for some composure before reopening them to shift to David, seeing the twinkle and what might just be a hint of promise in David's eyes.

Patrick shook his head ruefully and tossed several chips at Matt, who just snickered. David sat back down in his seat, glaring at

Matt with mock outrage. "Fucker!" he accused, planting a noisy kiss on Matt's cheek and swiping the chips Patrick had just thrown at Matt.

"Hey," Matt complained.

"I get a cut of any bet based on me."

"Damn it. Shot down again," Patrick muttered good-naturedly. "You better keep him happy, David, or I'll steal him away," he declared.

John and Jared actually chuckled, and John pointed at Trace, whose cheeks were flushing as he shuffled the cards. He couldn't help it. Just the thought of feeling David's lips on his neck again made him a little dizzy.

"You'll try," David shot back as he started dealing. But the cards went flying as Mabel thumped up on the table again.

"Whoa!" John exclaimed, barely rescuing his scotch glass in time.

"She can't stay away from you, David," Patrick said with a laugh as he started raking in the scattered chips.

"She's certainly Trace's cat," Matt teased with an evil grin. "Probably feels the same way he does."

Patrick, Jared, and John all turned expectant gazes on Trace, who cleared his throat and pressed his lips together, determined not to blush. "She might as well be David's cat," Trace muttered as Mabel settled down into David's lap again, where she started fastidiously licking at David's fingers. Trace gestured to her significantly.

Matt laughed. "Well, guys, David finally got some pussy."

All the men booed and threw chips at Matt as they got the cards back together. Trace still noticed glances sent his way but understood now that he'd been accepted by David's other friends. With a smile, he turned his eyes back to David, who had his cards in hand as he carefully rubbed Mabel's back from where his right hand lay in the sling. It was easy to smile while watching him.

The rest of the night was just as amusing and a little bit more charged, infusing all the men with raucous humor and teasing. While Patrick dialed back the intensity of his flirting, it didn't stop, and Trace realized it was just in the other man's nature. So he enjoyed it and the other guys' ribbing, especially when he slanted his own glances David's way.

"You're not as bad a player as you claimed, Trace," Jared said as they cleaned up. Trace sketched a bow, holding a tumbler of melting ice in each hand.

"Oh, I definitely expect you back in the game," Matt said with a chortle as he gathered his winnings. "We get the added benefit of David being too distracted to play as well as usual."

Trace's eyes widened a little, and he glanced to the kitchen, where David was directing Jared on putting the remains of dinner away and keeping Mabel away from the food.

"Oh, don't give me that innocent look," Matt said. "I watched you flirt with him all night after his little show of possessiveness. You did it quietly, but it was still there."

Pausing next to Matt, Trace felt a moment of nerves. He wasn't sure what he was getting into, only that it was exciting and new and felt different from anything he'd done before. He'd already acknowledged to himself that he didn't know if it was because he was such close friends with David already and the growing attraction was layering over that, or if it was just that David was a man. It worried Trace a little that he might be that shallow.

"Quit thinking so hard," Matt said quietly. Trace blinked and focused on him. Matt just smiled. "You're gonna be fine. He already loves you."

"Of course he does. We're best friends," Trace answered automatically.

Matt's eyes twinkled. "Of course," he replied tolerantly as he tucked the wad of bills into his wallet. "Hey, David!" he called out louder. "You need to make sure you have Trace here next time so I can win again!"

"That's the only way you'll ever win," David called back after Matt's taunt.

Matt was chuckling as he walked through the kitchen door, Trace following along. "I look forward to winning a lot, then," Matt teased. He gave David a careful hug and whistled as he walked out the door with Jared, the designated driver, who waved at Trace and David as he left.

Trace, glasses still in hand, was still staring after Matt as the man jogged down the steps. If Matt thought he'd be winning a lot, that meant he expected Trace would be around. Would he?

He was a little thrown by the immediate affirmative answer that leaped to mind. Not because of the fun to be had playing poker and hanging out, but because of the shiver he remembered feeling when David had cornered him in the kitchen, and later when he had kissed his neck in full view of the others. Trace felt a spike of desire in his groin.

Christ. If he felt like this around a woman, he'd be in the dining room, pushing her clothes out of the way for a hot fuck on the table right now, amongst the cards and chips, followed by a night of leisurely teasing and more pleasure in his bed.

"Whatcha thinkin' about?" David asked, stepping up to Trace's side, his chest brushing Trace's arm. Reaching out, he took one of the glasses but didn't step away.

Trace was honest. "You," he said with a smile.

David felt his skin tingle as goose bumps spread across his skin. Raising his healing arm, he stroked his thumb over Trace's cheek. He wanted Trace with a passion that he hadn't experienced in years. Placing his glass on the counter, he lifted the other from

117

Trace's hands, pulling the slightly taller man to him once their hands were free. "You need to tell me what you want," he whispered, lifting Trace's hair and stroking his neck. "I don't want to read something into this that you aren't offering."

Trace's eyes fluttered half-shut as David's soft touches heated him. "I don't know what I want, David," he admitted. "But it feels good. I don't want it to stop. Can't we just... see what happens?"

Pulling Trace even closer, until he was pressed up against his chest, David buried his face under the curtain of dark hair, his lips moving against Trace's neck as he talked. "Anything you want. Slow and easy. We'll see what happens." David licked from the hollow of Trace's collarbone to the sweet patch behind his ear. "God, you smell so good. I want to lick you all over." He realized his words were awfully provocative for a man who'd just promised slow, but it was the truth. Sucking softly at the tender patch of skin, he hooked Trace by his belt loop and pulled their hips together.

Purring deep in his chest, Trace burrowed close as he twined his arms around David's neck and tilted his head to the side in encouragement. "Slow and easy," he echoed, voice low. After another soft purr, he said, "You're seducing me, aren't you?"

David chuckled, a deep masculine sound that curled around low on their bodies and squeezed. "I was thinking that you were seducing me." Kissing and nipping at the offered neck, he rocked their lower bodies together in a rhythmic wave.

Trace gasped softly and lifted his hips against David's. "No, must be you. I'm not sure where I'd even start. Does what works on a woman work on you?" He shifted one arm to curl it around David's neck.

Stepping backward, David's hand trailed down to clasp Trace's, pulling him along as he led him toward the bedroom. "Let's find out."

Both Trace's brows raised in smiling disbelief. "I wouldn't be pulling you down the hall," he said with a laugh.

"You wouldn't?" David asked, his voice husky as he gathered Trace close again and leaned back against the wall in the hallway. "Then show me what you'd do."

Eyes flashing in interest, Trace took a steadying breath and stepped right up against David, only his hands on David's chest between them. He started to unbutton David's shirt as he first rubbed their cheeks against each other and then moved just enough for his lips to hover over David's, teasing. Trace moved his head slowly, almost sliding their lips together as he kept unbuttoning, knuckles purposely dragging downward along the warm skin of David's chest.

David moaned, the moist heat from his mouth mixing with Trace's. Nudging his chin up just a fraction, Trace played with the magnetic force between their lips, hovering so close but not quite touching. His nipples hardened to aching points as Trace dragged his shirt apart.

Trace hummed quietly as he slid one hand inside David's shirt to rub over smooth, warm skin until his palm covered one of those nipples. "Answers that question," he breathed, moving his palm in a slow circle.

"What question?" David gasped as Trace's fingers grazed the hypersensitive nipple. He'd already forgotten what he'd asked Trace to do.

Trace chuckled lowly. "My, my," he drawled. "Isn't that interesting." He shifted his face slightly to the side, teasing his lips along David's cheekbone.

David's eyes drifted closed as he lost himself in the feel of Trace's hands deliberately on his body. Trace. *My friend.* Trace. *My lover.* David's cock throbbed in his jeans, but uncharacteristically, he felt no need to rush. There was no hurry. Whatever was happening between them, they'd only have these moments once, and David felt nothing but anticipation and an eagerness to enjoy every moment. "More," he whispered harshly. "Touch me."

119

The warmth pouring off David's skin kept Trace close, and he let his eyes fall closed. The hall was mostly dark anyway. But he could feel. Trace lifted a second hand and slid it inside David's shirt as well, but made no attempt to pull the shirt free of David's pants or push it off his shoulders. This was exploring, and Trace was more than content to do exactly what David asked for and no more. It was powerful, knowing that it was his touch that aroused David.

His lips skipped softly along David's jaw while his hair tumbled forward to shield their faces. Their bodies were a bare inch apart. Trace could feel the quiet urge to push closer but ignored it. *Just see how it goes.* He dragged his fingertips across the tightened nubs, reveling in the rush he felt when David shivered under his hands.

David groaned, the muscles in his chest quivering. Swallowing, he rubbed their cheeks together, his nose nudging at Trace, begging for a kiss. Giving in to a desire he didn't know he had, Trace trailed one of his hands up David's chest and buried it in his hair while lifting his mouth to David's. It was soft and slow, first just their lips pressed together, before Trace dared to dart out his tongue to ever-so-slightly run along David's lower lip. David's tongue met his, tempting it into his mouth and sucking at it playfully. David's hands had been resting innocently at Trace's waist; now they ran up his sides and around his back to knead at the tight muscles under the soft shirt.

Trace sighed softly as he tasted scotch and David, a heady combination. His fingers lightly carded David's hair as he leisurely continued the kiss. When David's hands started moving on him, Trace groaned aloud and pulled away from the kiss.

"Oh hell. Start that and I'll do whatever you want." He arched his back slightly into David's hands. He adored a massage. Women who figured that out usually had him like putty in their hands.

"You will, will you?" David chuckled, nipping playfully at Trace's bottom lip and starting them down the hallway again.

"Come on then, Jackson. I'll trade you a back rub for a good-night kiss, but it better be a good one."

Trace laughed lightly as David walked him backward into the bedroom. "Mmmm. I'm getting off light," he kidded before pulling away to stretch. He hadn't realized he'd tensed up so much over the course of the evening. *Must be the stress of the unknown. Now I don't know why I was stressed.*

"Oh, I don't know. I'm expecting one hell of a good-night kiss." David reached for the small lamp beside the bed, clicking it on so soft yellow light filled the room, just enough to see. "Take off your clothes and lie down."

Trace paused and his eyes widened a little.

"I promise your virtue is safe in my hands. It just makes it easier to massage you," David assured him, anticipating Trace's reluctance. "I'm gonna go slip into my pajamas and grab some lotion. Care to finish undoing me?"

Trace's lips twitched as he paced over to David to unfasten his dress pants. He was starting to think it was an affectation—David had more than enough motion back in his arm to do up and undo his own clothes. But Trace didn't think he minded. "David, you've seen me in wet Speedos. That doesn't leave much to the imagination," he said wryly as his fingers slid inside the waistband and his knuckles brushed bare skin.

Unable to help it, David's breath caught as the tips of Trace's fingers grazed the head of his erection. Through clenched teeth, he rasped, "Yeah, and my imagination was certainly running in overdrive that day." Stepping back the moment his pants were undone, he turned from temptation. He'd promised Trace slow and easy, and begging for more of Trace's touch on his over-heated cock wasn't keeping his word. He momentarily contemplated jacking off as he shed his clothes but decided he'd rather draw out this exquisite torture and take care of himself after his kiss. On the other side of the door, David grinned, thinking of the times during the past two days when he'd felt Trace hard against him. Pulling up his pajama bottoms, he reached into the medicine cabinet for the bottle of massage oil.

Contemplating as David turned away, Trace rubbed his fingers together. He was fairly sure he knew what he'd touched, and he didn't want to think about it too closely. The idea of kissing another man: okay. The idea of touching his aroused cock? Trace swallowed and flushed, curling his hand into a fist. Disconcerting. Embarrassing, even, which in turn *really* embarrassed him. Intellectually, he knew there was nothing wrong with touching another man. Just wasn't something he'd thought about trying. *Until now.* It struck Trace then that David really wanted him. And Trace definitely didn't like the idea of teasing him. When the other man reentered the bedroom with a bottle of massage oil in hand, Trace had to speak up and clear his conscience. "David, is this a good idea? I don't want to get you all riled up."

David stopped next to Trace and reached up to smooth out the worry creasing his brow. "Does it bother you that I get turned on by your touch, your body, your kiss?" he asked softly.

Trace closed his eyes as David touched him gently. "No. That's a hell of a boost to my ego, actually," he admitted before reopening his eyes. "I… I'm just a bit wigged out about doing something *about* it. I know *I* hate a tease," he said frankly.

"You're thinking too much." David started to pull Trace's shirt out of the waistband of his pants. "I know who you are, and I know you've never done this before. I promised slow, and I intend to enjoy every moment of slow. If you get to a place you're uncomfortable, no harm, no foul. We can slow down, stop, back up, and just be friends. If it gets to be too much for me, I'll let you know. Okay?" Reaching up, he cupped Trace's cheek.

The look in David's eyes was soft and affectionate, and Trace turned his chin to kiss David's palm. "Okay," Trace agreed. "I'll try to stop thinking so much," he said, smile reappearing. He reached down to undo his pants, since David had already pulled his shirt loose.

Trace pulled off his shirt, draped it over the dresser, and got out of his pants. His hand trailed along the waistband of his underwear, but he decided against it. He totally believed David wouldn't push, but he was more concerned that he'd be too self-conscious to enjoy the massage. So Trace left them on and crawled onto the bed. "Okay," he said, wiggling to get comfortable.

"Chicken," David teased. Trace smiled ruefully. The boxer briefs clung to every dip and curve of his ass and upper thighs, effectively hiding nothing, and he knew it. But it was the principle of the idea. Trace snorted and shook his head, laying it down on the pillow he'd pulled under himself.

Kneeling on the bed, David straddled Trace's body, his weight coming to rest on the top of Trace's thighs. Reaching for the bottle of oil, he let his chest brush Trace's back. It was so much temptation. But he'd promised Trace slow and easy, and begging for more of Trace's touch wasn't keeping his word.

Now all this skin, these long legs and firm back and muscled arms, they were all under him, bare. *Someday. Someday I'll strip every stitch of clothing from him and make love to him like no one has ever before.*

Trace sighed as David got situated. "Get to work," he ordered.

David laughed, choosing to pour the cool oil directly onto Trace's back instead of warming it in his hands like he normally would.

Trace inhaled sharply and somehow kept himself from rearing back—not that he could go far with David's weight on his legs. "Thanks," he said sarcastically, though it was softened with a snorting laugh. "I'm real relaxed now."

"Yeah, well, don't piss off the masseur." David started to work the oil into Trace's back, moving it from where it had settled in the channel along his spine over the broad planes of muscle. He pushed deeply, feeling a slight twinge in his shoulder. He'd have to take it easy with his injured side and do the really hard kneading only with his left hand. Closing his eyes, he fell into a rhythm that was relaxing him as well as Trace.

"Mmmm, don't strain your shoulder," Trace murmured as David started to feel the muscles releasing the knots.

Not wanting a reminder of Trace's role as his caregiver, David worked as hard as he could at turning the tables—giving to Trace as passionately as Trace had given to him over the past month. A happy purr rumbled in Trace's chest as David worked.

Using his body weight as leverage, David rocked forward to press deeply into the meaty muscle of the other man's shoulders, his cock hardening as it pressed into the cleft of Trace's ass. Even through two layers of cloth, the touch was electric. Not wanting to make Trace uncomfortable, he immediately shifted back, sliding his hands down Trace's back to work at the muscles along the sides of his spine. But Trace drew in a long, slow breath, and his eyes fluttered open when he felt David lean into him, hard and long and unmistakable.

David felt Trace tense. *Damn.* He couldn't control his body's reaction to the sexy brunet; he simply desired Trace too much. So he was going to have to get Trace okay with it somehow. He leaned forward again, his body conforming to Trace's back, and whispered next to his ear. "Relax. I know you trust me. Just for a minute, don't think. Just feel." He pushed his aroused body unashamedly against Trace's ass. "*You* do that to me. You're sexy and beautiful, and it turns me on. I know you've danced with women, possibly even the wife or girlfriend of a good friend, and had your body react. Contact, touch, it tantalizes, teases, and my body responds. It feels good. Hell! It feels great. Even if it isn't going anywhere. If my touch brings you pleasure, and your touch brings me pleasure, just leave it at that. Don't make it any more complicated." David pulled the curtain of dark hair to the side and let his lips ghost over the back of Trace's neck.

Trace shuddered under David and obeyed, his muscles visibly relaxing. With David rocking slowly against him, Trace groaned and unconsciously shifted his weight. The longer David rocked slowly against him, the more Trace steadily grew more and more fond of it. It *was* arousing. He groaned and unconsciously shifted his weight off his own cock, which had hardened in reaction to David's compliments. Trace sucked in a surprised breath as his body reacted positively. David was right. It felt great.

Picking up the rhythm with his hands, David went back to the massage, letting his fingers mold Trace's muscles. His eyes shut and he bit his lip as Trace's hips continued to undulate in counterpoint to his movements. The fact that the erotic enticement was unintended made it even more provocative. The tension continued to build to the brink of climax, David's muscles trembling before he forced himself to slow the pace. Coming against Trace's ass wasn't a part of the slow seduction forming in his mind.

Practically melted against the pillows, Trace moaned in protest, and his hands flexed to grip the sheets. "David," he said hoarsely. *Fuck, he was so turned on.*

"Shhhh," David soothed, changing the massage to long, light brushes of his fingertips from shoulder to hip in alternating crisscross patterns. He could hear the need in Trace's voice and wanted so badly to offer to ease his ache, but he knew that Trace wasn't ready for that yet. He bit his cheek. It might hurt now, but losing Trace's friendship would kill him.

The light massage encouraged Trace to relax again, and slowly the arousal he'd felt at David's hands drained away as he got sleepier. All he knew was it felt incredible—and that David had aroused him so much he'd about come against the sheets. Trace pushed the thought away to mull over later. For now, he was just feeling.

David felt Trace's body release the last of the tension, sinking deep into the mattress. He continued to gently stroke Trace's back, shoulders, arms, and hair until the slow, even breathing told him Trace was asleep.

Carefully lifting himself off the bed, he snagged Trace's shirt off the dresser as he passed and walked barefoot into the living room.

Slipping the shirt over his arms but leaving it unbuttoned, he lifted the collar to his face, breathing in Trace's scent. His cock throbbed between his legs, leaving a spreading wet patch on the thin cotton of his pajamas. Stretching out on the couch, he slipped his hand under the elastic, pushing the pants down onto his thighs. Wrapped in Trace's scent, David quickly stroked himself to completion, Trace's name escaping on a breathy gasp as he came.

• Chapter 10

WAKING up slowly, Trace first became aware of being very warm, cozy, and happily curled up against someone. It didn't throw him at all. For several minutes, he dozed until his brain finally pointed out that he really should have been alone this morning. Frowning a little, very sleepy yet, and recognizing a bit of a hangover, Trace tried to remember.

David woke to a dull ache in his shoulder. He had moved to his back, he realized groggily, and his shoulder lay awkwardly on the pillow while the weight of a body was tucked up under that arm lying against his side. Remembering why he'd turned over, he opened his eyes, finding Trace so close that he could feel his breath on his face.

When his pillow jostled, Trace blinked open blurry, sleep-heavy eyes to see David very close, and he was so surprised he couldn't even move. David had shifted to his back, and his injured shoulder lay awkwardly on a pillow while the weight of Trace's body was tucked up under the arm lying against his other side. As Trace watched, David slowly opened his eyes, so close that Trace could feel his breath on his cheek.

It wasn't the first time they'd woken up lying against each other in the time that Trace had been staying with him. Apparently they were both cuddlers by nature, but this time, the incredible tension from the night before immediately crackled between them. Trace's breathing picked up as he felt himself tingle. Neither moved for a long moment, and then David began to close the distance slowly, clearly giving Trace plenty of time to roll away. He had absolutely no desire in him to do so as David brushed warm lips against his. Pulling away was the last thing on his mind. This was nice. It became more than nice as David licked at Trace's full bottom lip, sucking it softly. *Much, much better than nice, morning breath be damned.*

Trace's heart skipped, and his eyes closed unconsciously as he felt David's lips moving more against his with growing confidence. It didn't feel scary or wrong. It felt great, actually, with a little bit of surprising spark. Trace didn't want to move. He knew his lips were trembling as they parted slightly on a silent moan. *This is David.* Whatever happened, it would be okay. He unfurled his fingers to spread them across David's chest.

David's breath hitched as Trace's hand slid across his skin. It would be so easy to wrap his arms around Trace and start exploring, to figure out exactly what this was between them. When he finally pulled back, he gathered Trace closer against his side, resting their cheeks together.

It was comfortable, Trace realized. It made him wonder—was this what he had been thinking of in the car? Something warmer, something softer than just sex. He shifted his hand slightly, feeling David's warm and surprisingly soft flesh sprinkled with crinkly hair under it. His fingers were itching. Itching to stroke and feel and discover. He curled them into a fist. He wasn't sure what had gotten into him last night—or this morning. He could blame it on spending much more time with David than usual or it being too long since he'd spent time with an accommodating woman. But he wanted to touch. Touch David like he had in the car. And the look in David's eyes when he had opened them last night.... Trace had never seen a look like that from anyone directed at him. It had been scarily intimate at the time, enough to unnerve him and send him into the dubious safety of hard liquor.

But now, after a long moment of not moving, Trace shifted some more. His hand slid until his arm lay across David's ribs, and his head turned to use David's good shoulder as a pillow. He was huddled up close, and if he actually thought about it right now, he'd probably embarrass himself. Trace decided it was best to push thinking away for now. He just wanted this closeness. *Nothing wrong with that, is there?*

David shifted his arm to come up and rest along his back, probably to take the pressure off his injured shoulder. Trace actually went back to sleep for about half an hour before waking again with a sleepy sigh and burying his face against David's chest. This time he knew exactly where he was; he just didn't feel any urgency to move. David hadn't pushed him away, after all. Trace coasted his hand up David's ribs to tuck his fingers under his own cheek, letting the comfortable lethargy hold him in place.

David's heart raced as Trace cuddled closer, his mind too full to allow him any more rest. Of course, Trace would sleep 'til noon given the chance. David smiled and dropped a light kiss on the top of the dark head. They had learned a lot about each other, and apparently there was even more to discover. If someone had told him a month ago that he'd be sharing morning kisses with Trace, he would have told them they were insane, but somehow it just felt right, like a natural extension of the closeness—the intimacy—that had been growing between them.

Trace shifted again, and David frowned. An early riser by nature, he felt the need to be out of bed. His shoulder hurt, and he was craving coffee. He ran his hand up Trace's bare arm, hoping to coax him awake. He didn't want him to wake up alone and think David regretted their actions.

"Mmmmmm." Trace burrowed closer and hid his eyes against David's neck, shaking his hair forward to block the dim light coming through the blinds. "Still sleepy," was the muffled murmur.

David couldn't help but chuckle. "You are such a slugabed," he teased, attacking Trace's side with his fingers. "Half the day is gone."

Trace squawked and flailed, trying to catch David's hand. "No no no no no!" he practically squealed, handicapped because David was so close.

Oh, now isn't that interesting. Trace is ticklish. David grinned, sat up, and crawled half on top of the squirming man to renew his attack.

"Ack! David! Damn!" Trace yelled as he tried to wriggle away, but he was caught under the other man and held his hands back, conscious of David's shoulder. "I give! I give! Ack!"

"To the victor go the spoils," David announced, looking down at Trace beneath him and into sleepy eyes melted into liquid pools of chocolate brown with golden sparks. "Do you concede that I should be able to claim a favor of my choice?"

"Okay, anything," Trace said miserably, still shivering. "Just no more tickling, please," he begged. He gave David a pitiful look from where he was sprawled under him, hair a mess, face still soft from sleep.

Planting a hand on either side of Trace's head, David leaned down, careful to support his weight on his good arm. "I don't know," he mused, seeming to think it over. "You look good like this." He let his eyes take a long, lingering sweep over Trace's flushed face and chest. Mouth hovering dangerously close, David pondered claiming a "real" kiss—a kiss Trace would feel clear down to his toes and hopefully other parts of his anatomy. No, he decided. Trace wasn't ready for where David wanted this to go. When they went farther, it would be because Trace was so ready he was begging. Just the thought sent a slash of heat through him to connect to his groin, and he almost groaned aloud.

Trace studied David's face, his breathing and pulse calming. David's weight felt good, he acknowledged. Solid and squared rather than soft and rounded. He decided he liked it. Trace wondered if David was going to kiss him again. Trace wouldn't mind it. But…. "David?" he said, tone regretful. David's weight was right on his bladder, and that was a problem.

"I think I'll save my boon, but don't forget you owe me. I always collect." Grinning, David pushed himself off the bed. "I need coffee. Want some?"

Trace sighed in relief and climbed off the bed as well. "Yes. But not before I go to the bathroom." He scooted around David, but turned and hesitated, then impulsively leaned close to drop a light kiss on David's mouth before continuing on his way, pushing the bathroom door closed behind him. Once inside he let out a long, slow breath and raised a hand to touch his lips.

Chill bumps rose on David's skin after Trace's casual but intimate gesture. He hadn't had anyone who stayed around any amount of time in his life for years, and he missed moments like this—lingering in bed, making each other breakfast, casual displays of affection that somehow meant so much more than a fast and furious fuck. Forcing his eyes away from the closed door, David turned to start his quest for coffee. His mind was way too fuzzy to be dealing with the intense thoughts running through it. Thoughts like *I'm falling in love with my best friend.*

Once inside the bathroom, Trace let out a long, slow breath and raised a hand to touch his tingling lips. He found himself lingering in the bathroom—actually just staring in the mirror at his lips, feeling them buzz with warmth. This was so different from raw sexual attraction. He fucked that out pretty much every weekend, until just recently. But this? He knew he loved David; there was no question about that. They were best friends, and Trace treasured that. But he wasn't "in love" with David…. Trace looked up into the mirror with wide eyes.

Shaking off the rest of his sleepiness, Trace told himself to just cool it. There was nothing wrong with loving his best friend. That didn't mean he wanted wild and crazy man sex. He rolled his eyes at himself and sighed. "Jerk," he muttered. But those kisses had been awfully nice. *I wouldn't mind a few of those occasionally.* Laughing softly at himself, he wondered what David thought about those kisses. And he wondered if he'd get more soon.

TRACE hummed along with the sultry jazz music, shifting his weight back and forth along with the beat as he stirred the mix in the big pot he'd found in David's cabinet. He scooped up some of the liquid and pursed his lips to blow on it before he sipped it off the wooden spoon carefully.

David stopped in the doorway, watching Trace sway to the deep bass beat. The brunet and the jazz were a good match, both innately sensual. And he'd been finding out, in the past couple of weeks since the poker game, just how sensual Trace Jackson could be. Slight touches, barely there kisses, eyes wandering more openly over each other—just enough to keep David at a low simmer. He felt like a pressure cooker; every few days he had to get off in the shower just to keep from exploding on the spot when Trace gave him one of those innocent, smoldering looks. Only David was certain Trace didn't mean them to be at all that innocent.

"Something smells good," David said, walking into the room. He stopped and leaned against Trace's back, resting his chin on his shoulder. "Special dinner? Did you actually cook, or did you bribe one of the chefs trying to get into your good graces?"

"I made it myself, I'll have you know. I did bribe somebody to get the recipe, though," Trace said with a grin.

David nodded toward the pot. "Taste?" As he distracted Trace by nuzzling his neck, David reached around him to the counter and flipped some shrimp heads down to the floor, where Mabel promptly snarfed them up.

Trace lifted the spoon so David could sip from it. "Good, huh?"

A deep moan of approval rose from David's chest. "Excellent. But I'd expect nothing less." David grinned, shifting to lean his hip against the counter and watch as Trace spread a mixture of butter and fresh garlic on a loaf of bread. Trace wore a pair of faded jeans with holes in both knees and an ass that was so threadbare it was almost white. His T-shirt wasn't much better. It had been washed so many times that it was impossible to tell what its original color had been, but it clung to the muscular shoulders and arms enticingly. It was amazing, frankly, because David would have sworn Trace didn't even own clothes that old and beat up. Even his gym clothes were always neat and well-fitted. It was a very different look on him. A very *good* look on him, and David swallowed hard. *Pressure cooker.*

"Do you want some wine?" Trace asked, still swaying to the music as he reached into the cabinet for some glasses.

"Sure. I haven't had any pain meds today." Pulling the opener out of the drawer, he turned to the bottle sitting on the counter, cursing as he twisted the corkscrew with the wrong hand. "Damn!"

Trace sighed and walked over to take the bottle and corkscrew, pausing long enough to press a soft kiss to David's shoulder. "Well, you must be getting better if you get that far before it twinges on you," he said supportively, popping out the cork.

David rolled his eyes, leaning into Trace's side. "That doesn't help. I've been doing those damn exercises for three weeks now."

"Poor baby," Trace crooned, pouring the wine into two glasses. "How 'bout this?" Strong fingers gently probed the muscles of David's arm and upper back. The blond moaned, his head falling forward as the massage loosened the muscles he unconsciously held tight.

Leaning back into Trace's chest, David turned his head, kissing a line along Trace's jaw. "So, anything this poor cripple can do to help?" he asked, taking a sip of the rich gold liquid.

Humming with the music, Trace bumped their hips together, nudging David toward the stove. "Stir the gumbo. It'll still be another half hour or so," he said. "Do we want anything to go with it besides rice and bread?" he asked as he pulled a bag out of the cabinet.

"Ummm, we-ell...." David fluttered his eyelashes comically and puckered his lips.

Trace grinned and shook his head as he danced his way back over to David. "Hmmm. I don't know," he fudged. "Here I've been doing all the cooking, and you want dessert first?"

David's eyes widened innocently. "Appetizer?"

Rolling his eyes, Trace kissed David affectionately. "How's that?" he asked, amused. "Don't want to spoil your dinner."

David leaned his head back, closing his eyes and licking his lips like he was savoring a rare delicacy. "You're right," he said, opening his eyes and winking at Trace. "Far too sweet. Must be dessert."

Trace chuckled. "You sweet-talker," he accused lightly. "I bet you say that every time you kiss a food critic."

"Yep, every time." David grinned and went back to stirring the pot, brushing Trace as he walked past to fill the pot with water and start the rice. Just that simple contact kept him half-hard and incredibly aroused.

Snorting, Trace stirred unsalted butter into the water. "How many food critics do you know?" he asked, shamelessly fishing, which pleased David to no end.

Looking down into the bubbling liquid as though seriously inspecting the food, David replied evenly, "Just one." Trace smiled down at the rice, and after a few moments, bumped David's hip playfully before impulsively kissing the side of his neck, just below his ear.

Goose bumps climbed up David's neck and down his arms at the light touch. Trace being willing to accept his touch was one thing, but initiating them himself? David shook his head. He had no idea where this was heading, but it sure felt nice. They were so comfortable together and had so much fun. Trace was probably already the best relationship he'd ever had. Lifting a spoonful of gumbo, he blew the steam away and offered it to the man stirring the rice next to him. Trace puckered his lips to blow on the liquid a little more before sliding his lips around the spoon. He sighed happily. "A little more hot sauce, I think," he said, deliberately reaching in front of David and leaning into him to reach the bottle.

Purposefully not moving out of Trace's way, David maximized the drag of their bodies together. Oh, he was getting hungry all right, but he wasn't sure the gumbo was going to help. Trace chuckled as he pulled back and rubbed his knuckles against David's chest for a moment before opening the bottle and adding several shakes to the pot. "There we go. Nice and spicy."

David looked at Trace out of the corner of his eyes. He'd watched Trace flirt for years, but he'd never been the recipient of the attention, and it was doing amazing things to his libido. "Just the way I like it," he rasped.

Trace was flirting like crazy. He enjoyed seeing David get flustered over him. "Yeah, I figured," Trace drawled, bumping David's hip and rubbing for a few moments as another song started. He hummed along as he sidled down the counter to finish wrapping the bread in foil.

Pulling the spoon out of the pot and laying it on a plate to keep the stovetop clean, David followed down the counter, pressing the front of his body against Trace's back, fingers curling into his hips. "If word gets out you can cook, Jackson, I'll be beating them away from the door with a stick," he said, peering over Trace's shoulder at the fresh bread.

Trace chuckled. "Enjoy it while you've got it. I know you: living off takeout Chinese and drive-through crap. Yet another reason I have to take care of you," he teased, turning his head so he could kiss David's cheek.

"At least the Chinese has vegetables," David defended, sticking out his tongue playfully. His stomach chose that moment to growl. Looking down, he chuckled. "Will it be ready soon? I'm starved."

"Awww," Trace sympathized, rubbing the back of his arm against David's tummy. "Get out some bowls and put the wine on the table. We'll eat dinner. Then we can talk about dessert."

David's body reacted instantly to the potential for double meaning in that statement. A reaction he vigorously quashed, knowing full well Trace wouldn't be offering him the kind of dessert he was really craving and, if he were, they'd be skipping the dinner part altogether. Lifting the bowls down from the cabinet with his left hand one at a time for fear of breaking them, he set the table and poured more wine, carrying their glasses and the bottle to the table one at a time.

Trace gave the gumbo one more good stir, but he was preoccupied by thinking about the man moving around behind him. Actually, preoccupied with the thought of the "dessert" he'd mentioned. More kisses. More touches. The corners of his mouth tilted up. He was looking forward to it.

• Chapter 11

EYES riveted on the movie, Trace slid his hand toward the popcorn bowl, missing it altogether to rub across David's chest as his fingers hit the outer edge, and he paused, laughed, and started feeling around for the popcorn again. It probably would have been easier if he weren't half-draped over David, who was holding the bowl at his side away from Trace.

"Quit groping me. I'm trying to watch the movie," David teased, moving the bowl within easier reach. Truth was, Trace had picked a movie David had seen multiple times, and he was far more interested in watching the emotions crossing Trace's face than the TV screen.

"How did I miss seeing this?" Trace asked, chuckling as the pirate bemoaned the missing rum. "Have you had this all along and I just missed it?" He dug into the popcorn and ate it out of his palm, laying his head to the side against David's shoulder.

David tilted his head toward Trace, resting his cheek against the dark hair. "Yeah, I've had it since it came out. It's great for decompression." He shifted slightly, stretching his arm along the back of the couch.

"It's hysterically funny, is what it is," Trace said, snorting at the pirate's muttered comment about living with the woman. He shifted further on his hip to lie in the hollow against David's body, hand snaking up to steal the bowl of popcorn.

"Hey!" David poked Trace in the side.

"Ack!" Trace twitched and tried to cover his side with the bowl. He picked up a popcorn kernel. "Here," he said, holding it to David's lips.

"Oh no, I'm not so easily bribed," David warned. "If it was chocolate maybe...." White kernels flew up into the air as David's fingers attacked Trace's sides.

Trace flailed, trying to get away and stop David's hands, not doing too well at either. "No no no, please! Not with the tickling again! Jesus!" Trace squirmed, trying to get away from David.

"Please what?" David asked, looming over Trace and pinning the flailing arms at the wrist above Trace's head.

Trace tilted his head back and offered David a poor-pitiful-me look. "Please stop tickling me," he begged. "It makes me crazy. You know that!"

"Hmmm." David pretended to consider the argument. "What's it worth to you?" he asked, running his fingers up under Trace's T-shirt.

"A kiss?" Trace offered freely. As the weeks had passed since the poker game, a kiss had become more and more common*place*, yet not at all common, in Trace's experience. Each and every one felt special. He wasn't uncomfortable being so close to David anymore; in fact, he'd discovered that David was even better to cuddle with than a woman. He liked being wrapped up in David's arms, and he could also appreciate what David's touch did to his body. Every morning he woke up hard and aching, and every morning the idea of rubbing against David until he came sounded better and better. Trace chewed his bottom lip as he looked at David craftily.

David narrowed his eyes suspiciously. He knew that Trace was becoming comfortable with their kisses, but he still wasn't sure where this was headed. Stopping his fingers' torment, he leaned back on the arm of the couch, stretching one leg out on the cushions, the other resting on the floor. "I'll consider it, but you have to kiss me and I'll be the judge."

Trace scrambled up on his knees on the cushion, looking over at David. "So the kiss has to be good enough or I get tickled again, huh?" he asked, amusement twinkling in his eyes. He loved this teasing between them. It fed his own natural flirtiness. This was different from their normal hanging out from years past—and better. He scooted closer on his knees toward David.

A smug smile spread over David's face. "That's the idea."

"Hmmph. I've been told I am an excellent kisser, I'll have you know," Trace retorted playfully, shifting until he was as close as he could get without actually lying on top of the other man.

A sharp tug on his belt loops brought him crashing down on top of David. "So prove it."

Trace caught himself on one hand, but not before their bodies thumped together and his hair tumbled over his shoulder. He hummed in consideration, being challenged, and slowly pressed their lips together. It was a light, caressing motion. Smiling, Trace pressed more firmly, extending his tongue to trace along David's lower lip before he gently sucked that bottom lip between his own.

David's lips curved as Trace's caressed them, gasping as the kiss grew more aggressive. Angling his chin, he caught and sucked at Trace's tongue, his legs falling open and arching up as Trace's body settled against his groin.

Trace rubbed close, deepening the kiss into a hot, passionate mesh of lips and tongues. He raised one hand to delve into David's hair and hold him in place.

One of David's hands ran over the swell of Trace's ass and higher, slipping under the soft shirt and kneading the muscles of the broad back. Trace put all his effort into the kiss, groaning as he felt David's hands on him and his body's reaction. It happened faster every time. Sometimes David just had to look at him with that glint in his eyes and Trace's pulse sped.

Dragging his lips away from Trace's, David buried his face against Trace's neck, trying to calm his racing heart. Every time they touched, it got worse, harder to stop. David didn't want to pressure Trace. He was always excruciatingly aware that this was Trace's first time trying for a relationship with a man that was more than simple friendship, and he didn't want to do anything that would damage that friendship. It would be one thing if Trace wasn't as affected as David was, but he was.

David arched up against him, and Trace could feel the hard length of the other man's erection pressing against him. Head tipping back, Trace gasped as he felt David's thigh slide hard against him—against his now-hard cock—and his eyes rolled back in his head. "Jesus," he whispered starkly, and he shuddered as he shifted his hips to tentatively push back. "David, oh God...."

David's stomach flipped, a shiver traveling up his spine, his nipples hardening into tight peaks. How did you resist when the man of your dreams was lying in your arms making delicious, needy noises? He gripped the back of Trace's head with one hand and his hip with the other, holding him close but still. His lips grazing Trace's ear, he rasped, "If we're stopping, we need to do it right now. If we don't, I'm going to make you come. My hip. My hands. My mouth. I don't care...."

Every night since the poker game, Trace had gone to sleep thinking about David touching him—gently as they kissed, playfully as they tussled, distractedly as they worked, and passionately, at times like this. The idea was more than firmly set in his mind, and Trace was so turned on because the idea of David's hands, *David's mouth* on him made his head spin. "Please, David," he asked, lips grazing David's cheek as he pulled his head up to meet his eyes. Trace wanted the other man to know that he really wanted this. "Don't stop."

With a throaty groan, David's mouth crashed into Trace's, all gentleness gone from his kiss. This was claiming, possession, passion in its most elemental form. David's hips ground up again, his legs spreading wider, cradling Trace against the intimate juncture of his body. Trace felt swept under with David's kiss, swept off his feet, swept along with the wild current. He didn't want anything different. He gave as good as he got, arms curling around David as best he could as he moved against David's hips. The hard muscle of his thighs and the hard cock covered by denim were equally enflaming—David was as turned on as he was. Trace gasped against David's mouth and for the first time pushed himself hard against David to get more stimulation, choking out a soft cry as pleasure burned through him. Dear God. They were making out on the fucking couch like a couple of teenagers, and he was about to go up in flames.

Thoughts of flipping Trace beneath him, sitting him up and slipping to the floor between his knees danced on the periphery of David's consciousness, but he couldn't make himself stop the wild rush of erotic need that was building between them. David undulated under Trace, a shockingly perfect counterpoint to his thrusts, their rock-hard shafts rubbing along each other with every pass.

Moaning softly, Trace felt everything in him start to tighten so quickly that he was amazed; he had so much more control than this. But that all went out the window with David. Trace rocked harder, a soft whimper escaping as he bit down hard on his bottom lip. Almost. He was going to get off by rutting against his best friend. The thought struck through him like a shot of lightning, and suddenly he was that much closer to coming. "David," he whispered helplessly, pleading.

David's hand closed over the flexing muscles of Trace's ass, grinding them together forcibly, but it still wasn't enough. He wanted closer, harder, more…. He could feel Trace trembling under him, clearly just as aroused. "God," David ground out next to Trace's ear, panting. "So fuckin' close. Just touching you. Want to make you come, want to feel you come against me."

The words, combined with David's hands on him, pushed Trace to the very edge. He thrust against David harder than before, his pelvis rubbing constantly over David's length, each measure of its length and breadth drawing a gasp out of him. Trace released a low, tortured cry as he lost himself to it, just moving mindlessly, caught on the cusp of orgasm. He was shaking with it. His balls ached with it.

Writhing under Trace, David wanted to come, needed to come. "God! Oh, fuck…. Trace! Make me come. Make me come, baby," he babbled, his voice strained. "Harder…. God, like that. Fuck me!"

The pleading in David's voice broke any last reservations in Trace, and he shoved against David's groin, once and again and again. His breaths were harsh as his hands clenched hard, and then he froze in place for bare seconds before throwing his head back and crying out as he jerked against David unevenly, shuddering into orgasm. "David! Oh fuck, David!"

The tenor of Trace's voice reverberated straight to David's cock. He groaned, thrusting up into him over and over. "Trace!" he cried before biting into Trace's neck as his hips bowed off the cushions into the heavy weight of Trace's body.

Trace gasped as the flash of pain mixed with the climax rushing from his body, stealing his ability to breathe. The room was spinning, the edges of his vision going gray when he finally managed to inhale a gasping gulp of oxygen.

"Fuck, that was intense," David murmured sleepily after they had collapsed together. "Having you actually fuck me might be deadly."

Beyond caring about lying against David in wet, sticky jeans, Trace half-moaned, half-laughed, and turned his flushing face against David's chest. Every ounce of energy had left his body with his orgasm, and he was hanging in a state of suspended, sated, bliss. "I think I need to recover first," he murmured. "I'm stayin' right here," he added drowsily.

"Good." David's arms tightened around him, and they lay there for long minutes, just breathing.

When he regained his breath, Trace crossed his hands on David's chest and set his chin down on them, meeting David's eyes evenly. When he spoke, his voice was soft. "I didn't expect it to be so good," he admitted. He lifted his fingers and lightly traced along David's mouth. "I should have. You take care of me."

David brushed the compliment away, not quite comfortable with the intensity of what he was feeling. "I think you've got that backward. You're the one who's been playing valet and chief cook and bottle washer." His eyes skittered toward the TV just in time to catch the protagonists gazing at each other during a quiet moment. David had given up on finding happily ever after a long time ago, but Trace had him wishing again. That could be dangerous.

The change in David's tone nagged at Trace, and he shifted uncomfortably. If it were a woman saying those words, he'd think she was either embarrassed or regretful. He hoped that wasn't the case. He'd gotten swept up in the moment, for sure, but he didn't regret it. He would only regret it if it caused a rift between them. "Okay," he said softly, pushing himself up and scooting back, away from David, watching him carefully.

David felt Trace's withdrawal and unease more than he heard it and immediately made eye contact. His barriers low from the intimacy of the moment, he put everything he was feeling out for Trace to see. Reaching up, he stroked his fingers along Trace's jaw. "I'd like to take care of you, though. Will you let me?"

Turning his cheek into David's hand, Trace's eyes fluttered a little as he felt relief settle through him. David's eyes—they were so intense when focused on him. It made him feel like the center of

David's world. Trace had taken care of David without any thought of wanting something in return, but this? This was a step further into what was turning into something more than close friendship. Trace wanted it. When he spoke, there was more warmth in his voice. "Okay."

WHEN Trace blinked awake before dawn, he knew he had a problem.

He was half on his side, half on his belly, curled over David's side, his arm pulling the other man close, his head tucked into the curve of David's shoulder. Carefully he sat up, looking down at the other man in the dim light. Asleep, David looked younger—not that he was old, that little voice in Trace's mind insisted. The lines on his face softened, his lips a little fuller with warmth. Feeling swelled in Trace's chest and groin, the heat of growing passion warring with something stronger but quieter, a reflection of the strength of their friendship layered with growing affection.

It was the desire that niggled at him. Trace climbed slowly out of the bed, checking that he didn't wake David up. He grabbed shorts and a T-shirt and left the room, pulling the door closed. Slipping into the clothes, he headed for the kitchen and got a Coke out of the fridge. Sitting at the table, he pulled one leg up to brace his foot in front of him so he could prop his chin on his knee.

Their relationship was changing, and Trace had to admit he was scared. Scared and confused, enough that it had tinged his usually pleasant dreams with enough uncertainty that he was now wide awake and worrying over it. He took a drink and held the cold can to his forehead. Last night had been incredible. The flaming hot pawing and kissing and touching and explosive orgasms—Trace hadn't felt so satisfied after sex in a long, long time. Except now, he wanted more of it. More of it with David. And what would that mean to them?

Trace wasn't so concerned about the bisexual label; he was comfortable with himself and he was comfortable with sex in general. He was more concerned that what he had with David would flare and soon burn out, leaving them too uncomfortable to even be friends. The thought made his chest hurt so badly that he couldn't sit still, and he had to get up and pace, trying to shake the pain off. He didn't want that, not at all. He'd rather give up the newfound passion than have that happen.

After a few minutes of moving, he stopped at the sink to look out at the pinkish light starting to brighten over the backyard. What was he going to do? Sighing, he set the can in the sink and headed back to the bedroom. He stripped down, seeing no point in wearing the clothes to bed. Besides, he wanted the comfort of David's warm body against his. He slid under the sheet and scooted until he could wrap around the other man. After a few minutes, Trace was relaxed and warm and content. That had to mean something, he thought. Just being close to David made everything okay.

DAVID stirred, slowly waking, and shifted back into the heat of Trace's body unconsciously, murmuring a sleepy, "Mornin'." He kept his eyes closed, really wanting to stay asleep, but it just wasn't in his nature. As soon as he was awake, his mind started working, and this morning it seemed fixated on the feeling of Trace crawling back into bed. Rolling over and resting his head on Trace's arm, he asked, "Where've you been so early?"

Shifting to allow David to move, Trace opened his eyes slowly, focusing on the other man's face. "Just to the kitchen for something to drink," he said honestly. He lifted his hand and gently slid his fingers through David's soft hair where it lay mussed above his ear.

"Mmm," David hummed, closing his eyes to lose himself in the feeling of Trace's touch. "Did you start coffee?" he asked hopefully.

Trace's lips quirked. "Sorry. I was hoping I wouldn't wake you up. We were up late last night. This morning," he corrected. He kissed David's forehead lightly.

"Yeah, but I'm not complaining." Reaching up to run his fingers through Trace's hair, David rolled his body close again. "We okay?" he asked, voice hesitant. Last night had been surprisingly hot, but Trace's friendship was far more important than any sex, no matter how mind-blowing.

"I think so," Trace murmured. "I'm just... worried, I guess." His fingers slid down to trace the line of David's jaw. "Don't want to lose you *or* this. I'm just not sure how it's going to work."

"I could show you some videos... very instructional," David teased, rocking his body gently against Trace's hip. "Trace, you aren't going to lose me, but maybe we need to talk about what we're doing. If we are going to be serious though, I need coffee."

"Okay," Trace said softly. "You're very important to me, you know that? My closest friend. Never saw it coming that you might be my lover as well."

"Serious." David sat up, dropping a kiss on Trace's nose. "Coffee." He pushed himself off the bed and padded to the kitchen in his boxers, throwing back over his shoulder, "And I do know that."

Trace couldn't hold back the smile that pulled at his lips. Damn, he was a lucky man. Shaking his head, he climbed out of bed, pulled on a T-shirt to go with his briefs, and followed David to the kitchen. David was at the coffeemaker, carefully measuring the water and freshly ground beans.

Standing next to David until he'd finished, Trace leaned to kiss his shoulder. "I don't need any convincing," he murmured, sliding his hand along David's ass before going to the cabinet to pull out two mugs. "I know what I want and don't want."

A wake of tingles followed Trace's hand, swirling into David's groin and causing his cock to swell. Damn, that man was potent,

David thought, his eyes tracking Trace and watching the flex of muscles in his back and shoulders as he reached for the mugs. "If you don't need convincing, what do we need to talk about?"

Trace's movements slowed as he lowered the mugs to the countertop. When he turned, his face was serious. "If this doesn't work, or if it burns out, I don't want to lose you. I know how awkward a breakup is in a physical relationship. If it was us, it would tear me to pieces."

David moved closer as the smell of brewing coffee filled the room, just the scent clearing his head. "So we work to make sure that doesn't happen." Raising his hand, he placed it flat on Trace's chest. "Where do you see this going?"

Covering David's hand with his own, Trace searched his face. "As far as we want to take it," he said honestly, holding David's eyes with his own. "It probably sounds unbelievable, but I fit better with you than anyone else. And I'm not even talking about sex."

David's hand turned over, his fingers threading between Trace's. "We do seem to fit pretty well, don't we?" he mused, staring down at their joined hands. "I've never been as comfortable with someone as I am with you, but...." He paused, trying to find the right words. Trace had never shown any inclination toward men, and David already cared too much about him to be okay with this being a casual experiment. "Are you sure this is what you want? We can be friends. We can even be closer friends than we were before without adding the physical stuff. With someone else, I might be able to handle a little curious experimentation, but if we continue to kiss and touch, I'm going to fall for you." David fingers brushed Trace's cheek. He didn't add that he'd probably already fallen and if Trace walked away now, it was going to hurt like hell.

Trace's eyes half-closed as he turned his cheek toward David's fingers, rubbing against them longingly. "I want this," Trace said fervently. "I do."

The tight knot in David's chest released as he let go of the breath he'd been holding, waiting for Trace's answer. Running his hand along Trace's side, he curled his fingers into the loose T-shirt and pulled Trace closer. "Want this?" He nuzzled Trace's neck. "Or want me? I need to hear you say that not just any man could make you feel this way." He could feel Trace's cock growing against him.

Trace slid his arm around David's waist as he pressed close. "Want *you*," he said seriously. "David, no one's made me feel this way. No woman. Certainly no man. It's just you. I understand where you're coming from with the falling thing. I've never wanted to spend more than a few nights with anyone. They just didn't hold my interest. You had it before we even starting exploring each other."

"And this is pretty incredible," David added, nudging at Trace's chin and rubbing their cheeks together. "Try this with me?"

Smiling, Trace nodded and turned his chin to kiss the corner of David's mouth. "Not going to try. I'm going to *do*. With you," he said quietly.

A warm glow like good scotch spread through David's belly. "Yes," he murmured against Trace's cheek. Sucking the full bottom lip, he cupped the back of Trace's head, pressing their mouths together and teasing the seam with his tongue.

Trace hummed contentedly and relaxed against David, opening his lips and joining the leisurely kiss. He'd grown to adore David's kisses. He couldn't imagine a day now without at least three or four... dozen. Insane, he knew. Certifiable. But damn.... He shifted closer and pressed his groin against David's thigh as he curled one arm about David's neck and the other around his waist.

Everything in him was yelling that this was so right. He'd never felt that before, with a woman or man. He ached with the rightness of it. Maybe that was why it scared him. He'd never seriously considered making a commitment of any kind to anyone. But he wanted nothing less with David. He wanted to make this last.

"Why did we get out of bed?" David asked, trailing kisses down Trace's neck.

"You wanted to talk," Trace murmured as he let his head fall back, exposing his throat to David's lips.

"I did?" David groaned, accepting the offer of more skin with his lips and teeth. "I must be a fuckin' idiot. Talking is highly overrated."

"It really is too damn early to be out of bed," Trace agreed, voice faint as he shifted against David some more.

A low rumble resembling a warning growl rose from David's chest as his hands clamped onto Trace's hips, stilling the movement, but not pushing him away. "Keep that up, and we won't make it back to bed."

Trace sighed ruefully. "I am sleepy, though. Come on. You can keep me warm. At least 'til I fall back asleep. Please? Pretty please?" he wheedled, knowing how much David hated going back to bed in the mornings.

Stilling, David framed Trace's face with his fingers, staring deeply into his eyes. "I think I'd like that."

"Yeah?" Trace said, brown eyes brightening. "Good, 'cause my toes are cold," he said with a grin.

"Yeah." David turned the coffeemaker to warm, took Trace's hand, and led him back to the bedroom. Crawling onto the bed, he laid back on the pillows, pulling Trace close to his side. "I might just have to reconsider the whole 'sleeping in' thing if it feels this good," he mumbled, closing his eyes to just enjoy the feel of Trace so warm against his bare chest.

"Mmmm," Trace purred sleepily, already cozy and lying half on top of David, his actually quite-cold toes slid under David's calves. "Sleep now. Reconsider later," he mumbled, rubbing his cheek against David's shoulder. He still slept on the same side—the good side. It was easy to drift off now, knowing they were going to be okay.

• Chapter 12

"GOD, I will be so glad to be done with these damn visits," David groused as they arrived back home after his physical therapy appointment, a stop at a local bookstore, and a quiet, sit-down dinner at a nearby steakhouse they both liked.

"Well, you know it's doing you some good, and you only ranted for ten minutes about the sadistic therapist this time," Trace said as he parked the car, sparing a sideways glance for his companion.

David sighed and climbed out of the car. Yeah, it was doing him some good. He was hardly wearing the sling now, usually only after PT when he was tired, and tonight he wasn't even sure he needed it. "Yes," he admitted as they walked in the back door after Trace unlocked it.

Trace dragged in the door, sighed, and dropped his laptop and jacket on the small kitchen table. He yanked at his tie and looked down at his dirty and creased suit pants. "I think I am ready for a long, hot shower. Walking around the construction site of the new arena, I've felt dusty ever since." He glanced at David. "Or do you want to watch a movie or something first?"

But David only dimly heard him. After a long, sexually charged week of making out and exploring skin, he was more and more aroused just looking at Trace. And after the dreams of feeling the warm, velvet heat of Trace's cock in his hand or the taste of his come on the back of his tongue, he couldn't imagine a better place to quench the fire than a shower. With a very gorgeous and totally nude Trace.

"We could do that," David drawled, "but a shower and our clean bed would feel really good. I'd even promise to make sure you get nice and clean."

Trace chuckled. "Sounds like an excuse to get your hands on my naked ass." The smile on his face was clear. "But I suppose," he drew out, "that wouldn't be such a bad thing." He knew David was taking it slow, and that had so far included staying at least minimally clothed. He tipped his head to one side and looked David up and down. It would be a lovely sight, he knew, and David's toned body splattered with water...? Even more so.

David swallowed hard as he watched Trace unconsciously lick his lower lip. He knew that his growing feelings for Trace showed in his eyes—Matt had even commented on it—but he'd been careful to try to school his expression when Trace was actually looking, for fear of making him uncomfortable. But now, his barriers falling in the intimacy of the moment, he put everything he was feeling out for Trace to see.

And Trace didn't look away.

Silently, David took Trace's hand and led him down the hall. Walking into the bathroom, he flipped on the knobs, letting the water warm, and turned back to Trace. His hands played with the hem of Trace's rumpled dress shirt, letting his fingers brush the sensitive skin before lifting it over his head. Trace's thin undershirt soon followed. David's hands explored the smooth skin stretched over hard muscle, his mouth dipping to taste one of the dusky pink nipples.

Trace sighed and slid his hand over David's good shoulder, careful not to jar the other. Though it was well on its way to healing, Trace was always conscious of the injury and never did anything to hurt him. Unconsciously, he shifted to press up against David's mouth as his eyes fell shut. With the unspoken encouragement, David opened his lips and sucked the tiny nub into his mouth, grazing it with his teeth. Trace made a sound of pleasure deep in his throat, shifting his hand to curl into David's hair. His other hand wrapped around David's waist. "Cleaning me up?" he asked faintly, though he didn't object.

"Just getting started," David rasped, sinking to his knees and pulling at Trace's pants. Trace's hands rose to help, but he batted them away. "I'm taking care of you, remember? Consider it repayment for the dozens of times you've unfastened my pants. You can help me take mine off in a minute." His tongue trailed the line of soft hair down the center of Trace's abdomen, plunging into his belly button playfully. Trace's hand clenched on his good shoulder as David's mouth went lower. Trace's cock reacted by pulsing with heat and starting to harden.

David grazed his teeth against the hardening ridge, humming his pleasure at Trace's reaction. He desperately wanted to strip the man naked and lick and suck him clean and then some, and the way Trace was reacting, he was ready for it. Getting to his feet, he pushed the pants past Trace's hips and shifted toward the shower, adjusting the temperature of the water as Trace stepped out of his trousers and boxers.

After another moment of fabric moving, Trace stood before him, unabashedly nude. He'd never been ashamed of his body, and even if he were, Trace doubted he'd be hiding it under David's obviously appreciative gaze.

David had to swallow hard. Taking Trace's hands, he lifted them to his chest. "Undress me," he whispered.

Trace had swallowed hard at the temptation of David's mouth on his body, regaining his equilibrium when David didn't go ahead. That would have been mind-blowing, Trace was sure, but he wasn't sure how he would react afterward. Embarrassed, most likely, because he was sure he'd balk at returning the favor. He reached for the button on David's jeans, sliding his fingers inside the waistband to pull it apart and then lower the zipper. This he could do: easy touching. He wouldn't have hesitated to stroke a woman at this point. He rubbed his knuckles against David's swollen flesh.

Unable to bite back the groan prompted by Trace's touch, David leaned heavily against the wall, his knees shaking. Even the simplest of touches from Trace affected him more than the blatant sexual overtures of his past partners. Wrapping his fingers in the long dark hair, he pulled Trace close for a kiss. Sighing against David's lips, Trace slid his hands over David's hips to push the jeans down, then the warmed cotton underneath, down to his thighs where David could reach. He was faintly nervous about stepping forward. He'd lain all over David with them clothed. How would it feel with just heated skin? He wasn't shy, but….

Their mouths met over and over as they stroked one another, familiar enough with each other that every touch was a pleasure. David shook loose of his pants, his hand coming forward to rest on Trace's bare hip, the pad of his thumb brushing the hollow in lazy circles. The kiss continued at a slow and easy pace that belied the pounding of the blood in his ears and various other parts of his body. Trace slowly relaxed, slightly humming against David's lips in approval.

"Let's get in the shower," David urged. *Before I suggest we skip it all together and just go to bed,* he continued silently.

Trace opened his eyes and nodded, turning to push open the glass doors and step into the water. He could feel David's eyes lingering on his broad tan back, which tapered down to narrow hips and the paler skin of his ass. Stepping into the shower, David ran his hand over the lighter skin, cupping the lower curve and squeezing. Trace couldn't help but grin at the back wall. David was groping his ass. He reached up to change the shower massage setting to more of a gentle rain than the driving water now shooting out.

He had stopped under the water, but David kept moving forward until the front of his body was pressed to the back of

Trace's. Reaching around him with both arms, David grabbed the soap and a washcloth. Lathering the cloth, he set to work, running it up and down Trace's chest as his lips trailed across Trace's shoulder and up his neck. Shifting his weight, Trace simply relaxed back against David. It was sexy as hell, feeling David's hard, muscled body against him, feeling David's cock rubbing against him. Despite the warm water, he shivered as warm lips coasted across his skin, and he reached out to touch the tiled wall beside him.

"Turn," David suggested as his hand guided Trace to stand with his back against the tile. Starting with his arms, David carefully washed every inch of Trace's skin from his shoulders to his hands. Lifting the clean fingers to his mouth, he sucked at the water dropping from their tips, his eyes never leaving Trace's.

Trace knew he had been right, as far back as three weeks ago at the poker game. He *was* being seduced, and he was *loving* it. He lifted his other hand to touch David's lips with his fingers. This was getting so erotic he was afraid he wouldn't be able to see straight. His body slowly reacted, recovering from before and getting really interested again. David's touch spread like fire. It was addictive. Trace wanted more, and he tilted his hips to rub his cock lightly against David's thigh.

David's hands—one covered in a washcloth and one bare—skated up through the slippery suds, over Trace's shoulders and down the hard planes of his chest, circling his nipples. He sank to his knees as he moved the washcloth lower on Trace's body. Taking his time, he washed Trace's swelling length until it stood out, proud and erect, from his body. Moving the soapy washcloth between Trace's legs, David rolled the tender sac in his hand as he let the running water rinse the rest of him clean. Just like he had with Trace's fingers, David's tongue reached out and lapped at the drops of water running down Trace's cock, blue eyes turned up and burning with hunger.

Already groaning with pleasure, Trace leaned his head back against the wall and watched the cloth move over his body. He tried to control how rapidly he was breathing, but any thought of control was shredded when he saw David lean forward and extend his tongue to slide lightly along his sensitive, aching cock. He choked on David's name, and both hands flew to bury themselves in David's hair, turned dark by the water. There was so much he wanted to gasp out, but it all sounded dirty in his head, and he didn't want it to be that way. Trace just whispered, "Please," with passion burning in his eyes.

Letting the satiny head stroke his lips, David hummed, licked, and sucked Trace's cock from tip to base. Dragging his tongue up the underside in a long, slow swipe, he flicked it rapidly at the juncture of the crown, sucking the length into his mouth when Trace's hips bucked forward. Soap-slick fingers continued to explore and play with the heavy sac and all the sensitive skin they could reach.

"Oh sweet, sweet baby," Trace breathed as he just slightly pushed in and pulled out of David's mouth. He was afraid to do more—both because he'd never done this with David before, and because he was practically on the edge of coming already because it was happening at all.

David grinned, and Trace knew he'd been caught trembling. But he was no blushing little girl, even if it was his first time with a man, and he pulled David's head slightly forward. David cupped Trace's ass, pulling him forward with a hard, fast rhythm. David swallowed until Trace's cock was moving past his lips and down his throat with each stroke.

"Oh *fuck*," Trace swore as his fingers grasped about David's skull and his hips started snapping forward. It was too, too incredible to resist, and Trace couldn't stop. Dimly he had the thought that he'd never been able to fuck a woman's mouth like this; the couple times he'd tried hadn't gone well. But not only was it going well, David was driving it, encouraging it.

Trace's uninhibited response was incredibly arousing. Reaching between his own legs, David formed a loose fist around his cock, pistoning his hips forward into the channel.

"Shit. David...." Trace gasped, feeling his balls draw up hard as he tingled all over. "David," he mewled, turning his face up into the water. He'd been afraid of this, though he couldn't for the life of him remember why.

Pulling back long enough to speak, David moved his hand from Trace's ass to his cock, to continue the insistent pace. "Come for me, Trace," he rasped, his abused lips swollen and red. "Let me taste you." His fingers curled back around the swell of the tight ass, the tips grazing the deep cleft. *One step at a time, Carmichael,* he chided himself. On another day, he'd show Trace the wonders of pressure on his prostate. Of course, that didn't mean he couldn't.... His hand stroked down his own cock, already about to burst, cradled his balls, and probed a single finger against his own entrance. It'd been so long since he'd been fucked. He whimpered.

David's hand on his ass didn't even register as the pleasure bubbled over inside Trace, and he started to shake. Knowing it was important, he kept his eyes open, watching David. The sight hit him like a ton of bricks. David's right hand pumping his own cock as his lips whispered over the swollen head of Trace's, his eyes closed and face contorted with what looked like bliss; his left hand was down between his own legs, thrusting up into himself. Trace had an image of what David must be doing and just like that, he snapped and growled as he slammed into an intense orgasm, keeping glazed eyes on David the whole time.

David swallowed repeatedly, suckling and licking the pulsing length as Trace continued slow, shallow thrusts into his mouth. His own peak was really only a touch away, the steady, circling pressure he'd been teasing his prostate with keeping him just on the verge. Letting Trace slip from his mouth, David looked up, moving his good hand to his cock.

"Fuck," Trace panted as David pulled back from sucking him.

"Now you're relaxed," David drawled as he lapped at the drops of water dripping from Trace's cock.

"Relaxed...." Trace moaned as the fire faded.

"Watch me," David rasped. "Watch what you do to me."

When he reopened his eyes, it was to see David focused completely on him, one hand between his own legs, his other wrapped around his painfully hard cock. Eyes clouded with satiation and heat, Trace sagged against the tile to keep his balance as he kept watching David. If he could get hard again, he would, Trace thought a bit wildly as he lifted a shaking hand to wipe the water from his face. Just seeing David lick and lap up his come.... He twitched as another flash of heat tore through him. "Do it," he said hoarsely. "I want to see."

Trace watched David's left hand twist as his body clenched down on his fingers, and several tight strokes on his cock later, David was coming, crying out Trace's name before he collapsed forward, his forehead coming to rest on Trace's thigh. His body shuddered around his fingers, increasing the intensity of his climax. "Oh, fuck. Trace!"

Watching him as his entire body shuddered in climax was one of the most erotic sights Trace had ever experienced. His breath hitched along with David's, extending the orgasm's high.

David gasped, trying to settle his breathing. "Damn. Damn," he panted, pulling his fingers free and grabbing the soap, letting the cooling water carry away the traces of his climax.

Trace petted David's hair, his shoulders, his back, the side of his face. He could feel the hot exhalation of breath on his thigh. He was amazed they could wring these types of reactions from each other. Leaning just enough to the side, he shut off the shower. He groaned as he straightened and slid a little against the wall. "I'm not sure my legs want to hold me up anymore," he murmured, fingers still stroking David gently.

"Yeah, one of the advantages of being the one on your knees," David said cheekily, attempting to get to his feet.

Snorting, Trace looked down at David. "So how are you going to get up off the shower floor?" he asked, eyes twinkling. It was a very nice view from his vantage point. Damn, but David was a fine-looking man.

"My friend with the shaky knees is going to give me a hand," David said, reaching up with his good arm.

Trace grinned and leaned down a bit to grasp David's arm and help him stand, and when they both shifted to regain balance, they ended up right against each other. Thinking about it for only a couple of heartbeats, Trace leaned to brush his lips against David's.

David grinned against Trace's mouth, sucking the moisture off his lips. "You taste as good up here as you did down there. I should take showers with you more often." Pushing open the door, he stepped out, yanking a towel off the bar and tossing it backward at Trace. "Let's get dry and go lay down. I'm getting cold, and the clean sheets I saw you putting on the bed earlier are calling me."

The intimate words still threw Trace for a loop, but he liked them and the way they made him feel. He caught the towel and started drying off. After tonight, he was wiped out as well. "That was incredible," he murmured, leaning over to kiss David gently. Although he knew it was silly, he was a little edgy about how David might react. Deciding not to worry, he hung up the towel and kissed David's cheek as he walked by to go out to the bedroom.

David watched him walk past, biting his lip. There were so many things he wanted to say to Trace, but he just didn't think the other man was ready to hear them yet, if ever. Walking toward the bed, he didn't bother with boxers or pajamas, sliding between the sheets, moving his legs over the cool, crisp cotton. "Mmmm," he hummed sleepily, automatically scooting toward Trace's warmth. Of all the things he would miss when Trace went home, the cuddling would be missed most.

Trace always started out on his side when he slept, though invariably he ended up on his belly half-across David. He shifted his arm to let David scoot over close and then hugged him as he yawned sleepily.

"Night," David mumbled, burrowing into Trace's chest.

"Night," Trace murmured, warm, sated, drowsy and comfortable. Even the fact that this was the first time they'd slept together nude didn't faze him. His fingers stroked David's shoulder erratically, and he drifted to sleep with his lips curved in a satisfied smile.

• Chapter 13

"C'MON, David. Poker is tonight, and the guys decided on casual instead of work clothes, but your idea of casual might get you mistaken for homeless," Trace called out from the bedroom. "Don't you have one pair of jeans that are still intact? Or maybe a pair of khakis?"

"Oh, and what are *you* going to wear, fashion plate? I will not let you out of the bedroom in the *one* pair of jeans I've seen you wear," David yelled back from the living room. *Hell, no.* Those jeans showed off far, far too much of Trace's seriously sweet ass.

"I've got khakis and a T-shirt," Trace claimed, distracted as he dug through another drawer of folded clothes.

"Well, I've got jeans," David stubbornly called back, not budging from his comfortable spot on the couch, Mabel curled up happily in his lap.

"I can't find one clean pair, and dirt may be all that is holding some of these threads together. If I wash them again, they may disintegrate!"

"Will you quit yelling and come in here?" David shouted in the general direction of the hall. "And what are you doing going through my clothes, anyway?"

Trace appeared at the end of the hallway. "Trying to put away the laundry I did last night. I swear I have no idea how a man who is supposed to be at home healing up goes through so many clothes." He pointed an accusing finger at David. "And you never put them in the hamper. If you did, I'd have washed them with the other clothes last night. So you have nothing but suits hanging in your closet, gym clothes in your dresser, and a couple of drawers of stuff Goodwill wouldn't even take at this point. You've got nothing casual to wear, and I *didn't* find any clean jeans."

David scrunched up his nose. "Try the third drawer down in the bureau."

"That's where the sheets are," Trace replied, frowning. Why would he look there?

"Yeah, well, check in between the sheets, then." As soon as the words were out of his mouth, David started laughing.

Trace crossed his arms, shook his head, and sighed, aggrieved. He was going to get David dressed nicely in something besides an off-the-rack suit for work if it killed him. A smirk escaped as he ran his hand over the gathered hair at his neck and disappeared back down the hall.

David wondered all of a sudden why his cheeks were aching. Then he realized he was smiling so widely it was a wonder he didn't strain something. They sounded like a serious couple, lovers committed through and through. He bit his bottom lip. *That's what I want.* Just a week ago, on his knees in the shower, he'd found out just how much he wanted Trace, and the intimacy between them was growing every day.

"You *cannot* be serious!"

David turned his chin to see Trace again emerging from the hall, a pair of jeans hanging by a belt loop from Trace's long finger. "Those are my favorite jeans!" David claimed.

"These jeans are worse than my jeans," Trace said, absolutely sure David would get arrested for wearing these jeans in most cities. That, or propositioned.

"They are not. They're perfectly decent," David insisted.

"Uh huh. Then put them on and show me how decent they are," Trace suggested, swinging the jeans back and forth on his finger.

David met Trace's eyes, lips twitching. Those pair of denim jeans had been washed and washed and washed and washed over the years—Wranglers really lasted. He'd had that one pair of jeans since college. *College.* Not that he'd admit that to Trace. Besides, he was ridiculously proud of the fact that he could still fit into the damn things. There was no way he was getting rid of them.

"David?"

Blinking away his thoughts, David huffed and shifted a protesting Mabel onto the couch so he could stand up. He stripped down to nothing—Trace's brow was climbing, but David never wore anything under the most comfortable jeans in the world—and walked over to Trace to pull the jeans out of his hands, step into them, pull them up, and carefully rotate his shoulder forward so he could do up the button fly.

Trace cleared his throat, eyes very wide as they took in the sight of the very soft, very snug, very well-fitted jeans that fit David's body like a tailored glove. "Jesus," Trace breathed. Now *his* pants were very well-fitted. Too well-fitted.

David raised an eyebrow. "What?" he asked. He watched intently as Trace's tongue extended ever-so-slightly to moisten his lips as he walked in a circle around David.

"You're proposing wearing these jeans around the guys?" Trace asked. He didn't like that idea at all. While he knew Matt wasn't a threat, he wasn't too sure about Patrick.

"Sure," David said with a shrug. "Wouldn't be the first time." *In fact, Matt was with me when I bought them.*

Trace reached out to cup David's ass firmly before spreading his fingers over the faded fabric, following the curve of a muscled, lean buttock and sliding two long fingers into a mass of worn threads barely holding together to stroke bare skin. "It's not that I don't like seeing your ass," Trace drawled as he pinched, "but I'm not sure I want to share it with everybody else."

David slowly smiled. "Is that so?" *Fuck. Just the thought of Trace feeling possessive....*

Trace's hand covered the very well-defined bulge in the front of David's jeans. "I think you like that," he murmured. "Like knowing that I don't want to share?"

"Yeah," David admitted huskily. "I like it."

Trace moved to stand in front of him, hand still on David's ass, and kissed him gently. "I think I do too."

David swallowed hard as the sexual tension zinged between them, and their bodies leaned together like one magnet attracting the other. Trace squeezed again and stepped back.

"That's settled then," Trace announced.

"Settled? What's settled?" David asked, feeling a bolt of panic. He was *not* getting rid of his jeans.

"You need some casual clothes. New jeans, a nice pair of khakis, maybe a pair of walking shorts," Trace said with a nod. "We're going shopping."

Then the panic really struck. "Shorts! But Trace," he almost whined. "Shopping? Not the mall on a Saturday! It'll be full of teenagers performing their ritualistic mating dance."

"That's okay. We'll muddle through." Trace reached up with both hands to catch David's face. "Because you're not wearing those jeans, got it? They're indecent."

"I'll show you indecent," David promised as he reached for Trace, but Trace edged away just enough.

"C'mon. Sooner done, sooner home and I might—"

"Reward me for putting up with the mall," David finished, already looking forward to it.

Trace just smiled. He had plans for David, those jeans, and a little hands-on fitting.

"DON'T spill the salsa," David warned when Matt bumped him from behind as he topped off the bowl. He hadn't seen his friend approach, but he could hear Trace still talking to the others in the dining room, and Matt was the only other guy present comfortable enough with full body contact. David wondered exactly when he had started unconsciously keeping track of Trace's whereabouts. It probably had something to do with the unrelieved sexual tension from their shopping trip.

It hadn't been nearly as horrid as David had predicted, thanks in no small part to Trace's touchy-feely tendency to grope him every time they stepped into a dressing room. Unfortunately the trip had taken longer than either of them had expected, and there had been no time to do anything but pull out the snacks for the game and give the living room a cursory straighten before Matt had arrived, the other guys close behind him.

"I see Mabel has made herself right at home." Matt laughed as Patrick cursed the "flea-ridden furball" and tossed her off the table for the umpteenth time. She seemed to think that poker chips had been invented just for her amusement.

David grinned, glancing over his shoulder into the other room, his eyes catching Trace's and warming.

"Her owner too," Matt drawled.

"Yeah." David dragged his eyes back to the block of cheese he was slicing. There hadn't been time to make dinner before the guys arrived, so they were having a cold buffet on the fly.

"Yeah? That's all you have to say? Come on. Things have obviously progressed beyond the bi-curious stage."

David felt his gut tighten. "Oh, he's still curious…."

"So?"

Normally David had no problem sharing personal details with Matt, but he was reluctant to share what was developing between him and Trace—as if close examination would damage it in some way. "Did I thank you for giving me a push?" he asked instead.

Matt stared at him for several drawn-out moments. "No, but I'm glad it's working out. It has been too long since you've had anybody special. I could wish he worked for a different paper and rooted for a decent baseball team, but other than that, he's damn close to perfect."

"It's been a while for you too." David watched his friend shift. Matt usually diverted serious conversations with humor, but his glib comeback didn't materialize.

"Longer than I care to acknowledge. I think I'm past the stage where I'm going to make that connection. Too old for anyone to look at seriously." Looking over his shoulder, he watched Mabel stick her paw into Trace's glass, as if she was trying to fish something out of the scotch. "Maybe I should get a cat."

David snorted. "That'll be the day. A dog, maybe, but you are *not* a cat person."

"Dogs are too much work."

"Which is exactly why you don't have a boyfriend." Putting down the knife, David reached up and tugged at Matt's collar. "People take work, too, and they don't sit at home just waiting for you to walk through the door so they can shower you with love."

"Exactly what is wrong with them!" Matt smirked, disappearing behind his shields again, and David wagged a finger at him.

"You guys in this hand or not?" Patrick called from the other room.

"I'm in," Matt answered, retreating before David could continue their conversation.

David sighed and scooped the cheese and crackers onto the crumb-covered tray. He briefly considered if Matt and Patrick might make a good pair before deciding that they'd kill each other in a week. *What was it about being in love that made you want everyone in your life to find someone too?*

David stood there at the counter and stared at the food. *In love.* He loved Trace, very much, and he didn't know if he should say something about it. What if it was a deal breaker? What if Trace's desire to explore what was between them extended only as far as friends and lovers without the step to actual commitment? David groaned. He knew he was just nervous in general about their relationship. Trace had given him no reason to doubt how good they were together.

Picking up the tray, David moved to the doorway to the dining room and his eyes connected with Trace's as he moved around the table to his chair. Trace's heated gaze was stripping the new clothes from his body, and David let the buzz push his worry aside. *Now if I can just survive until it is a reasonable time to shove these guys out the door....*

• Chapter 14

DAVID hummed happily, setting the casserole dish on the stove, ready for the oven. He'd cheated and bought a tray of manicotti from his favorite Italian restaurant, but when it came to cooking, he figured the end justified the means. Matt had dropped the food off at lunchtime with only a minimum of teasing about having to deliver David's traditional "date dinner." David couldn't quit thinking about Trace coming home. He laughed softly at himself for being so domestic. He'd gotten approval from the physical therapist to do three half-days at work next week and couldn't wait to share the news.

Hearing the door open, David called out, "I'm in the kitchen!"

"'kay!" Trace answered.

David listened to Trace's footsteps and plastic rustling heading back to the office—to hang up the dry cleaning. But when Trace didn't appear after a couple minutes, David headed down the hall. Trace was standing there, looking at the moderate amount of clean clothes—his—that had started stacking up on the shelves in the closet, gnawing at the side of his thumb.

"Did you get lost?" David asked from the doorway, watching as Trace stared into the closet. Walking up behind him, he wrapped his arms around the slender waist, propping his chin on Trace's shoulder. "You should have told me you had dry cleaning. I had them deliver mine this afternoon. They could have thrown in yours and saved you the trip."

"It was no trouble," Trace said, covering David's hands with his own. He turned his chin to kiss David's temple.

"I got good news today. They released me to go back to work."

Trace frowned. Already? Just like that, he was healed up and ready to go? "You aren't ready for a full—"

David put a hand on Trace's chest. "Not full-time and I still can't drive, but Attila the Hun said I could start back half-days next week."

"Would that be Attila the therapist or Attila your doctor's nurse?"

"I obviously need to find some new slurs." David laughed. "The physical therapist."

"Does he know how much typing you do?" Trace asked, still not convinced. He glanced to David's shoulder with another frown.

"Eh… what difference does that make? It is all hunt and peck anyway. One-handed or two, I'm slow as molasses."

Trace sighed and pulled David into his arms and brushed a light kiss over his lips. "I'm proud of you. You've been working really hard on your exercises and it's paying off. I know you've been getting stir-crazy. I'm just worried it won't be totally healed up and something will happen to hurt it again."

"It'll be fine." David laid his head on Trace's shoulder. "It would have been a lot harder without you around to keep me sane." Threading their fingers together, he pulled Trace toward the door.

Trace slid the closet door closed. "I've accumulated a ton of stuff over here. It's going to take multiple trips to get them home again. I bet you'll be glad to fill this closet back up with all that junk you took out to make room for me," he said, poking fun at David's pack-rat habits.

David stumbled, Trace's hand immediately steadying him. He'd been so happy about having Trace in his life that he'd been living completely in the moment. He had no idea what Trace might be thinking of for the future. "Uhmmm, yeah." His stomach fluttered in a strange way. "Dinner is almost ready if you want to eat," he managed to choke out around the lump in his throat, his own appetite completely gone. How could he have not considered that Trace would be thinking of leaving?

The tight sound of David's voice worried Trace, and he turned to see the other man's frown. "Hey, what's this?" Trace reached up to rub the furrow on David's brow. Had David gotten as attached to him as he had to David? "Don't you want your house back to yourself?" he asked curiously. "Don't think I'm leaving *you*; no way that's happening," he asserted as he gently pulled David back against him.

Looking up into the clear brown eyes, David sighed, relaxing slightly. He could understand Trace wanting to go back to his own home, his own routine. He'd just have to deal with it or do his best to convince him to stay. "It's going to feel pretty empty without you. I got manicotti from Angelo's."

"I love Angelo's," Trace said with a grin. He kissed David lightly and rubbed their noses together. "C'mon. Quick shower, and then feed me," he said, taking David's hand and pulling him toward the kitchen. "'Cause then I have plans."

David picked the conversation right back up when they were at the kitchen counter forty-five minutes later. "I hope those plans involve me getting you hot and sweaty," David purred, letting his momentum press Trace into the counter when they reached the kitchen.

Trace hummed happily as David pressed up against him. "Oh yeah," he said throatily, nipping at the other man's neck. He groaned as his belly cramped with need. "We better eat fast, or I'm gonna hit my knees right here."

God, he wanted to. He'd not tried it yet, but he'd slowly been coming to the realization that he wanted to. He'd tasted David on his fingers, and he'd held him in his hand. But he wanted more. He wanted to see David come apart just like David made him fall to pieces. Or he'd at least like to try to make it happen.

David trembled at that husky promise, his nipples and cock hardening instantly. His hips rocked forward against Trace's leg; his hands went sliding down to cup the curve of his ass and pull him closer. "You'd really...? You want...?" He swallowed, unable to finish the sentence with the images flooding his mind.

Nodding and rubbing his cheek against David's, Trace slid his hands to grip David's upper arms as the images flooded his mind. "Yeah," he said huskily. "Wanna try. Want to make you feel what I do when you do it to me."

A chill raced up David's spine. Dinner was highly overrated, and wasn't pasta always best reheated anyway?

Trace's hand dropped down to caress David through his jeans, reminding him of the serious groping that had gone on in the dressing rooms at the mall. David groaned and moved his hips against Trace's hand as his heart pounded. It was enough to make something snap inside Trace.

Trace groaned and moved his hips against David as his heart pounded faster. "Okay," he breathed. "Dessert first." He lowered himself to one knee, his hands dragging down David's body. Once on both knees he turned David's hips so the other man leaned back against the counter and started to unfasten his jeans.

David gulped, looking down at his lover. "Trace? Trace!" he said, tugging on Trace's shirt.

Heated brown eyes shifted up to glance at David. With his lover's surprised tone, Trace felt calm descend upon him. He smiled sweetly and nuzzled David's thickening cock through his boxers. "Yeah?"

Exhaling a stuttering breath, David sagged slightly as his knees went weak. "Can we? I want…. Not in the kitchen." His eyes darted toward the door, incapable of coherency with Trace's mouth that close to his cock.

Trace tipped his head back. "Okay," he said agreeably. He climbed to his feet. "What do you want?" he asked, leaning in close to kiss along David's jaw.

"You," David sighed. "God. You. Bed or couch. Don't care, but I need to sit down before my knees give out."

Chuckling, Trace took his hand and led the way into the hallway heading toward the bedroom. "I sure know that feeling," he said wryly. At the side of the bed he pulled David into his arms for another heated kiss, plunging his tongue into the other man's mouth in as close a claim as he'd ever made. He wanted David so badly.

David whimpered, melting against Trace's body. If he'd been aroused by his friend before, it was nothing compared to the way the world was spinning now. Trace taking control made David's entire body throb.

Feeling David give in to him was heady; David had always taken the lead, ever since they'd begun exploring each other, simply because Trace wanted him to. He'd had so much to learn about pleasing a man. But now, now he wanted to be the one in charge. He jerked David against him, hard, grinding their groins together as he kissed the other man hungrily. "Gonna blow your mind," he growled before biting hard at the juncture of David's neck and shoulder.

David's head tilted of its own accord, a soft mewl escaping. *You already have,* he thought, glad that the mattress supported the backs of his wobbly knees. At least when they gave out, it wouldn't hurt. "You touch me and I melt," he whispered harshly, his lips nudging inside Trace's collar to lick at his chest.

Trace purred and tilted his head back to give David more skin to kiss. "We're even then," he breathed. He moved his hands from David's hips to his belly and finished unbuckling his lover's belt.

Clothes. Clothes were definitely a hindrance. The thought penetrated David's pleasure-fogged brain and his hands started to work on untucking Trace's shirt. "There ought to be a rule against you wearing clothes in the house," he muttered, cursing as his fingers fumbled with the small buttons.

Laughing breathlessly, Trace pulled open David's jeans and shoved them over his hips before yanking at his shirt, sending a popped button to the floor. "Your house, your rules," he said, leaning in to suck David's earlobe between his teeth.

"Oh, I like the sound of that," David purred, gasping as Trace's teeth tightened. "Do that to my nipples, and I'll be your slave for life."

"How can I resist an offer like that?" Trace whispered, pulling the sides of David's shirt farther apart, sending more buttons flying. His mouth surrounded the nub of skin, sucking and biting at it.

"Ah, fuck," David cried, sinking to the bed and pulling Trace with him. Trace clutched at David, refusing to let go of his prize as he suckled at his chest hungrily. He landed on top of David's knees, and his fingers plucked at the other nipple in a promise of what was coming.

A strangled sound of pure need broke from David's throat, his body bowing, seeking more contact from Trace. He blinked his eyes rapidly, trying to focus. "I want you inside me tonight, Trace," he rasped, trying to catch the warm brown eyes of his lover. "If you don't want that, you need to tell me now."

Focusing on his lover's face, desire flared inside Trace and he felt a surprising sense of possessiveness. It was fragile and new and made him feel shaky, the idea that he would want David to be his and no one else's. It was a feeling he'd truly thought he'd never experience, to want someone so totally. Something about David must have flipped that switch inside him. "I want it," he breathed, wonder clear in his voice, before he lunged forward with all his eagerness to capture David's mouth.

David's legs parted, drawing Trace closer and cradling him against the most intimate part of his body, and he sank into the kiss. This felt so good, so right. He wanted to beg Trace to move faster and savor every second at the same time. Unwilling to part with the lips on his, he settled for running his hands down the broad muscles of Trace's back, cupping and kneading his ass to silently urge him closer.

A low growl rumbled in Trace's throat as he kissed David thoroughly. When he pulled back, his lips were red and swollen. "Want to taste you," he said, shifting his hips to rock against David's groin. "Want to kiss you. Want to lick you up and down and feel you shake because you know it's me."

The room spun and David's body trembled right on cue. "God, Trace." He clutched at Trace's sides as the brunet carefully stood up before going to one knee and pulling off David's shoes and jeans.

Trace shuffled between David's knees and leaned to press his cheek against the thin cotton that covered his lover's cock. As he inhaled, he realized he wasn't nervous. He wanted this. He turned his chin to mouth David's erection through his briefs, breathing against the fabric hotly.

David's knees fell open limply, his eyes rolling back in his head. "Trace," he panted, his hips arching off the mattress. "Can't... gonna make me come."

Chuckling, Trace nodded, rubbing his lips along the line of David's cock. "That's the idea, lover," he purred, avidly watching David's reactions. He started licking and sucking at the covered flesh, soaking the cotton with his tongue until he found the blunt, swollen head. Acting on instinct, Trace closed his mouth over it.

Surprised, David cried out, his face flushing at that outburst. He wanted to be cool and controlled, but Trace stole every ounce of restraint he possessed. He'd honestly never thought he'd feel Trace's mouth on his cock, no matter how much he wanted it. His eyes fixed on the tongue and mouth working over his cock and every sensation was amplified tenfold. The unpracticed but enthusiastic touches were the most erotic thing he had ever experienced. "Fuck, fuck," he chanted blindly, his hips lifting in sync with Trace's lips. "Move—fuck—move the…." He broke off to catch his breath. "Want to feel your mouth on me," he finally managed to choke out.

Trace's eyes closed as he shuddered. To think he reduced David to this. Holy hell, it felt incredible. He raised his mouth from the wet fabric and looked up at his lover, seeing the surprise and desire there. David was so gorgeous like this. Heart pounding, Trace smoothed his hands over the briefs, and his fingers slid into the waistband to pull them down and over the swollen cock. With one last glance at David's glazed eyes, he leaned to simply slide his lips along the soft skin of David's erection.

A thousand pinpricks of sensation fired from the area brushed by Trace's mouth. "Oh yes," David hissed, his fingers sinking into the silken strands of dark hair. He collapsed back at an awkward angle against the headboard, limp. With an irritated grunt, he shifted sideways so he could lie back against a pillow, pulling his legs up onto the bed.

Trace followed, kneeling between David's thighs, giving his lover the same treatment he had through the briefs, sliding his cheek and stubbled chin along his cock, lightly licking along its length, mouthing its girth before finally lapping right at the distended head with a soft purr.

David squirmed. He'd never gotten off on so little, but it felt like Trace's tongue was pulling directly on invisible lines leading down into his balls. With every upstroke, his body contracted and threatened to spill onto Trace's tongue. He attempted to stifle a sharp cry as Trace teased and circled the head of his cock, failing miserably and giving in to a throaty moan as the lips closed over the swollen tip. Lifting slightly, he rocked up into the intoxicating heat just slightly, unable to hold still.

Trace wanted nothing else at this moment than to please David. The noises and movement set his own cock to aching, but he wasn't willing to give up. He just hoped he didn't hurt David somehow. Lifting one long-fingered hand, he wrapped it around David's cock and squeezed as he began to suck carefully. He wanted to hear more of those cries. The taste was stronger than off his fingers, of course, but Trace decided he liked it. He liked anything and everything about David. Trace wanted to feel David moving under him, driven mad by his touch. His pulse pounded. He still remembered what David had said. He wanted Trace inside him. Trace moaned deeply at the thought of it as his groin contracted in pleasure, and he felt David's cock harden a little more and extend farther into his throat. It was throbbing slightly against his tongue.

Trace's groan sent shivers skating over David's skin, hardening his nipples to painful points and making his cock pound. Unaware, he reached up to rub at the puckered nubs on his chest to ease the sting, planting his feet and pushing up into the tight fist. His eyes flickered open. Looking down at the full, red lips stretched around the shaft of his cock, David couldn't hold back. "Oh God. God, Trace!" he gasped, gripping his lover's head, not to push himself deeper but to make sure he didn't. Hips stuttering, he tried to pull away from Trace's mouth without losing contact with his hand. "Fuck! Coming!"

Surprised by the strength of David's thrashing, Trace pulled his mouth off his lover's cock not quite in time and the come dripped and smeared on his lips. Gasping at the sheer eroticism of it, Trace tightened and moved his hand as he extended his tongue to catch the next splatter that hit his cheek. Delighted laughter bubbled over as another thin stream hit his chin, and he wiped at it with the back of his hand. *He* did this to David. *He* did it. Oh *Christ*! That kernel of him wanting to claim David as his own swelled and popped ecstatically, and Trace had no idea what to do or think about it.

The force of the climax that hit him left David with no option but to hold on and ride it out. Hips bucking, eyes clenched tightly shut, fingers wound in dark hair, he chanted Trace's name over and over as his body shuddered and surged. When the intense pulses subsided into gentle twinges, he opened his eyes, seeking reassurance that his lover was all right. Trace stared at him, eyes glowing with stunned happiness and desire, flushed cheeks and swollen lips painted with his come. David came close to climaxing again. Instead, he pulled Trace down with a throaty groan. "Mine."

Trace's answer was a weak whimper as he shivered at the passion riding him, and his lips slid wetly over David's. David felt the same way. Maybe there was nothing wrong with it, then. "Yeah," he breathed. "Yeah." He let go of David's cock and slid his hands up to cup his face as they kissed with open mouths, and he tried to clamber up into David's lap, hungry to be closer to his possessive lover.

Sitting upright, David pulled Trace up to straddle his lap, his hands roaming feverishly, his mouth only leaving Trace's long enough to speak. Breathing was optional at this point. "Not good enough," he complained, trying to situate their two long frames against each other. "I want you laid out in front of me."

Trace let out a long breath as he shifted under David's hands with a soft moan. "I am so fuckin' turned on by you," he said huskily as he rubbed his palms over his own chest, fingers sliding under his hanging-open shirt. He reached up to shove his hair off his shoulder and met David's eyes with his own, which flashed with serious want. "What are you gonna do about it?"

David leaned forward, following the arch of Trace's neck with his lips and then his tongue until his mouth hovered next to Trace's ear. "I'm gonna lay you down and explore every inch of your skin with my hands and then with my mouth. I'm gonna compare the taste of your skin here," David licked the sensitive hollow behind Trace's ear, "with the way you taste here," he ran his thumbs into the crease between Trace's leg and body, stretching the fabric tight against Trace's cock. "Let me taste you, make you so hard you tremble, and then show you what it feels like to be inside me."

176

"Aww, hell," Trace hissed, eyes wide as his body twitched so hard he thought for a second he was going to come right then and there. He dropped one hand to press over his groin, trying to relieve a little of the pressure and get control of himself. "You better be careful or I won't make it to the inside part," he said shakily. "Christ, David. You really want... want me to...?"

A low chuckle rumbled in David's chest, and he pressed his grin into Trace's shoulder, the joy inside him expanding to the point that it had to bubble over somewhere. Grabbing Trace's ass, he pulled him closer. "Yeah, I really want you to...." His words faded out as he stared into Trace's mesmerized eyes. For some reason it just sounded totally wrong to blurt out the word "fuck." Wrong and harsh and lewd. But how else could he say it? "Fuck me. Make love to me. Come so deep inside me I can taste you." He emphasized each statement by rocking their hips together, feeling his spent shaft begin to twitch with interest as it brushed against Trace's hard bulge.

David's words caught Trace hard in the gut. Make love to him. *Yes. Oh yes, I want that.* The rest just made his head spin. "You're gonna have to help. I know what's supposed to happen, but no hands-on, you know?" he rasped.

Just the idea of being Trace's first male lover was enough to harden David's cock completely. He'd not recovered this quickly in years. "I'm sure you'll figure it out, and I'll guide you every step of the way." Rolling off the bed, David opened the curtains, letting in the bright light of the full moon. "Take your clothes off and lie down for me." He pulled open the nightstand drawer, getting the supplies they'd need and putting them close at hand.

Swallowing hard, Trace shrugged his shirt off and let it drop as he stared at David, lit by moonlight. How could he express how gorgeous this man was to him? And he was going to make love to him. Trace didn't want to just fuck. He wanted more. His pants pooled at his ankles, soon joined by his briefs and socks, and he stepped away from them as he pulled the band out of his hair, shrugging it over his shoulders the way he had discovered David liked it. Trace crawled onto the bed and shifted to lie on his side, facing David. His hands itched, and he grasped the sheets.

David pushed Trace onto his back, crawling over him. "My turn," he growled, his mouth attacking one of Trace's nipples, sucking it strongly until it peaked high enough to catch it with his teeth. While he sucked, he let his thigh push Trace's erection into his body, bracing himself on his arms and sliding up and down.

Trace gasped and lifted against David, his chest, then his hips, begging with his body for more. He clutched at his lover's shoulders and moaned luxuriously as he breathed David's name. Obviously his lover wanted him, maybe even wanted to keep him? Trace shivered as he figured out that was the way he felt too. David's hands traveled up Trace's side, pulling his arms up over his head and trapping both wrists in one hand. His mouth moved to the other nipple, his body continuing to undulate, keeping Trace on edge but not providing enough friction to push him over.

A strangled whimper tore from Trace's throat as he lightly pulled at his arms, just enough to feel restrained, not with any intention of breaking free. The dominant gesture sent heat shrieking through him, and every touch of David's tongue fanned the fire. "David," he gasped out. "You keep this up, we won't make it to the inside part."

"Wimp," David teased lightly. "You tellin' me you can't get it up more than once a night? That's not the story I've heard told all over town." Spreading Trace's thighs with his knees, he ran his cock directly against the heavy balls and rock-hard length.

"Jesus!" Trace swore, jerking up against David, his hands curling to dig into David's upper arms. "You're about to find out," he said as he felt the tension curl tightly in his groin. "And I wanna know who's talking about me!" he added breathlessly.

"Everyone. Everyone, my love," David purred, sliding down Trace's body. "If they could see you like this, they'd...." David shook his head, not even wanting to think about someone else touching Trace. "Wound up like this, I could come just watching you, but I'd rather make you come." Lifting the cock from Trace's belly, he licked at the head with a broad swipe of his tongue and swallowed the entire length in one long pull.

It wasn't David's voice or what he wanted; it was the endearment hidden in there that snapped what little control Trace had left. His lover's mouth closing around him just made it that much more inevitable, and he choked and keened with each pulse of his orgasm, his grip on rational thought spiraling out of reach.

David swallowed every drop, continuing to suckle his length as he pushed Trace's knees open wider and up toward his chest. Allowing the half-hard cock to drop from his mouth, he looked up from between Trace's thighs. "Remember how I took my time cleaning you in the shower and I said I was going to taste you everywhere?" he asked with a devilish grin. "There is one more place I need to taste." Leaning back over Trace's open and vulnerable body, his tongue lapped at the tight sac and lower.

Trace's dazed eyes widened as David dipped his chin down and dragged his tongue over his lover's balls and farther. All Trace could manage was a whimpering gasp as he curled his fists in the sheets. *Christ*, he thought, *it doesn't get more intimate than this.* He shivered and moaned.

Every inch David could reach, he sucked and licked, swirling his tongue around the puckered entrance and nipping at the pale cheeks. He watched as Trace got hard, his cock lengthening along up his belly. David pressed his lips tight to the small opening, sucking and moaning as the muscles under his hands trembled. His tongue flicked over the pucker, pressing just inside, leaving the hole twitching and wet. "I want to put my finger in you. Show you how good you're about to make me feel. Trust me?" David murmured against the velvety skin.

Dragging open his eyes to look down at David through the heated haze that enveloped him, Trace squirmed a little as he drew a steadying breath. "I do trust you," he said, reaching to slide his fingers along David's cheek. "You always take care of me."

"Pay attention because you get to do this to me next," David said, reaching for the bottle of lube. Coating his fingers liberally and drizzling some directly on Trace, he licked at the underside of his cock, sucking it back into his mouth just as the tip of his finger slipped easily into Trace's body. With plenty of lubrication, his finger glided smoothly in and out of the tight muscle.

As a finger slid into him and circled in and out, Trace sighed and let his eyes flutter shut. He wasn't surprised when the push of David's finger didn't exactly hurt—David knew just how to tease him, thrusting in and out or gently rubbing, fingers sliding so smoothly along Trace's cleft, laving his aroused cock, soaking in the heat radiating from Trace's skin.

David flicked his tongue over the head of Trace's cock, and he curved his finger to stroke Trace's prostate—eliciting a keening cry.

Trace was shocked when the rub of David's snub fingertip left a trail of fire that flared so hot he cried out before he could even think to stop it. "Holy hell, David! I'm supposed to pay attention with you doing that?" he asked, incredulous.

"God, so responsive." David groaned and shifted on his knees between Trace's legs as he slid his finger in again, twisting gently, trying to send Trace up in flames. He grinned after letting the cock in his mouth slide free, the vibrations of suppressed laughter dancing up and down the shaft. "No, not really. Thinking really isn't the goal at this point. Just feel for me, baby." His finger continued to tease as his words grew low and throaty, his tongue randomly licking at the cock in his hand. "Having you inside me will feel ten times this good. And coming," David moaned. "Coming.... You inside me, clamping down around your cock." Trace's muscles tightened around David's finger, and he moaned again. "God, Trace."

"Jesus," Trace breathed, pulling his knees up. The mix of swirling sensations was confusing and arousing at the same time. He knew full well what it felt like to be inside a woman, even one who was small and tight. He'd been in a woman's ass too, which was a huge turn-on. But being inside David could in no way possibly be the same. He felt himself contract around David's finger, and another bolt of pleasure shot through him. God, was this just a taste of what it would be like to have *David* in *him*? He twitched as his cock throbbed. "David," he rasped. "I need you."

David crawled up Trace's body, trailing kisses along a path until reaching Trace's mouth. "So take me, lover."

Curling his arms around him, Trace rolled them until he lay atop David. He stole another long, wet kiss before scooting back to kneel between David's thighs. His eyes raked over the firm body laid out before him, and he leaned to kiss David's belly before taking up the bottle. At the sudden rush of nerves, he reminded himself that he knew what he was doing. *Intellectually.* He spread some lube on his fingers and slid them under David's balls, rubbing as he went. Trace didn't break eye contact as he rubbed over the hole he was going to bury himself in. "So hungry for you," he whispered.

An erotic chill spread across David's skin. Planting his feet on the mattress, he lifted into Trace's touch. "Want you inside me," he rasped, drowning in his lover's eyes. Swallowing hard, Trace pressed against the portal and slid his finger in slowly to the second knuckle, as deep as he dared.

"Oh fuck! Deeper!" David cried, his eyes fluttering. It had been so long since he'd been this intimate with anybody and knowing it was Trace was driving him crazy. He could read the reluctance in Trace's eyes and the way he was biting his lip. "You aren't going to hurt me. Remember the feeling of my finger in you. Let me show you," he soothed. Reaching between his legs, he slid a long finger in next to Trace's, guiding him deeper and helping him find exactly the spot that made him see stars.

Trace watched his finger sink inside as David guided him, and he felt David's body twitch when the side of his finger rubbed over a bump. For a long minute, and several strokes later, he felt his lover's body clench around him. "Okay?" he asked, glancing at David for approval.

David nodded. "You ready to do this?" he asked, voice unsteady. "Because I'm gonna come, and I really want you inside me."

Sucking in a breath, Trace tilted his head back for a moment as he gathered himself. "Yeah," he murmured. He grabbed up the condom, rolled it on, and slicked himself with a soft moan. Then he shuffled closer between David's thighs. His hands shook as he lined up, pressed against the pucker, and started to push, fumbling a couple times until his lover's body opened to accept him. He stopped immediately, biting his lip, his free hand clenching on David's leg.

"God, don't stop!" David's hips tilted up, his hands pulling Trace deeper. Gasping, Trace obeyed, starting to rock slowly in, the motion familiar even if the body wasn't. Once far enough inside, he slid both hands to clutch at David's spread thighs. David's body bowed, wanting Trace deeper, closer. Reaching up, he hooked his hand around Trace's bicep and pulled. "Kiss me," he begged, wanting to be connected to his lover in every way possible.

Trace moaned as he carefully laid himself down and leaned on his elbows, licking at David's lips before kissing him. He felt like he was caught in a slick, hot vise, and he didn't want to leave it. The heat was boiling in his veins, and the urge to move was undeniable. He kept shifting his hips even as he lay atop his lover. When they finally parted to draw breath, Trace whispered, "So, so good," in an achingly tender voice. It was overwhelming, being a part of David this way. It was so much more than he'd ever hoped it could be, and he hadn't even realized he was hoping at all.

"You, inside me. Nothing ever felt this good," David moaned, his hands traveling up and down Trace's back, kneading at the flexing muscles.

Humming softly in agreement, Trace pushed himself up further on his elbows, arching his back as he made a first, long thrust on a soft gasp. He looked down at David intently as he slid in over and over until their hips bumped. "David, I had no idea," he murmured. Trace's hair poured over his shoulders, swaying with each move, and he licked his bottom lip as he tried to keep his concentration on not peaking too quickly. He wanted this to last.

David swallowed, hypnotized by the man moving above him, inside him. "Me either," he croaked, throat dry. "And I don't even have the excuse of never having done it."

Trace chuckled breathlessly. The even motion of pushing himself forward into David's body with his knees was somehow even more maddening than the hard, sharp thrusts he fought against. "Feel so damn close to you," he murmured, ducking his head to draw his tongue along the line of David's throat.

"Can't get any closer, and I'm not sure I ever want you any farther away." A particularly well-placed thrust caused every muscle in David's body to tense, his thighs trembling. His hand slipped between their bodies.

Lifting slightly to make room for David's hand, Trace shifted his weight back and thrust in a little harder, groaning each time their bodies clashed. His chest tightened with that indescribable sense of possessiveness—this man was *his* lover. *His.* Thrusts strengthening, Trace gritted his teeth against the swelling orgasm. His hands gripped David's hips, holding the other man's legs on his forearms. "Touch yourself, David. I need to see you come, knowing it's me driving you to it," Trace bit out, a little bit of greediness riding him so hard he couldn't escape it.

David's hand closed back around his erection. He was so close that it wasn't going to take long. Watching the emotion in Trace's eyes, hearing the passionate tone of his voice, feeling him tremble, David groaned, fisting himself rapidly, wanting to feel Trace's climax almost more than his own. He could see the love in Trace's eyes, and shaken, David ground out, "More, harder, something, please!" as everything in him tightened and he felt like he'd explode. He took the last couple of hard thrusts as Trace's moans filled his ears, and the same overwhelming pleasure swamped him.

Trace tensed all over as his orgasm slammed into him, almost unexpected—he'd thought he'd have another minute—and he gave a long, quiet cry over each shift of his hips as he came. He was shaking, lost to the feeling, a feeling he hoped he'd never have to give up. The realization only made the shockwaves more acute as he moaned David's name, heart aching.

The uninhibited pleasure washing over Trace's face was all David needed to push him to the precipice. "Oh my love," David breathed, finding just the right grip on his cock and jerking twice, forcing a wild cry out as everything went white. Stilling his hand, David let the last strokes of Trace's cock send him over. "Trace!" he cried. Then David's pants turned into soft whimpers. "Oh Trace, oh baby… coming… coming!" And he came, hard, one shot, and then another, and another yell as he abandoned himself to the pleasure.

Twitching through the tapering climax, Trace managed to pry open his eyes to see the ecstasy written on David's face. *Christ. He's so gorgeous.* "So gorgeous," Trace murmured, dragging one hand down his lover's chest as he watched him shudder through the aftershocks of his orgasm.

Pulling Trace down on top of him, David wrapped his arms and legs around the solid body. Breathing too hard for a deep kiss, he buried his face in the crook of Trace's neck.

After a few minutes, a short sigh accompanied Trace's cock slipping loose of David's body. "I need to clean up a little," Trace said. He kissed David's forehead and climbed off him to sit on the edge of the bed. After a few breaths, he headed into the bathroom to get rid of the condom. He cleaned up and took a wet washcloth with him back to the bed. He turned the bathroom light off and stood there, caught in watching David in the moonlight. The fierce possessiveness had waned, and now he wondered if it was just a spur of the moment thing. But the strong affection remained, that was clear.

He joined David on the bed and shook him gently. "Hey, aren't you hungry?" he asked as he started wiping off David's belly.

David sighed heavily, as if put upon. "Yeah, actually, I am. Don't want to move, though." He turned a satisfied smile on his lover. Trace straightened, setting his hands on his hips. He looked awfully satisfied as well. His hair still floated around his shoulders in a mess.

"Angelo's? Manicotti? Wine? Cuddling on the couch?"

"Mmmm. Sounds better and better," David said. "You convinced me."

"Well, c'mon then," Trace said, lightly smacking David's ass as he walked out to find some comfortable clothes.

"Watch it, Jackson! You might want this ass undamaged later!" David called after him, a huge grin on his face.

Half an hour later, they were sitting close on the couch, eating the pasta and a salad Trace had tossed. David watched him, knowing the whole falling thing was moot. He was so far gone on Trace he didn't even want to consider looking back. Trace made a sound of pleasure, setting his empty plate on the coffee table and leaning back. "I love Angelo's," he purred. His eyes shut as he rubbed his belly.

David laughed. "You ate it fast enough," he said, glancing down at a whole piece still on his plate. He'd been so busy watching Trace that he'd stopped eating halfway through his plate. "Want some more?"

"Yeah, but I'm too lazy to go get it," Trace drawled.

"Here," David said. He scooped up a bite and held the fork to Trace's lips. The other man opened his eyes and blinked, then opened his mouth. David deposited the bite on his tongue with a grin.

"Mmmmm. Now this is pampering," Trace murmured after swallowing.

"You worked hard this evening; deserve a reward," David answered, offering another bite. Trace replied by taking the bite and humming happily.

The manicotti didn't last long, nor did the wine, and David took the glasses and plates to the kitchen. When he returned to the living room, he grabbed both of Trace's hands and hauled him up.

"What?" Trace asked with an ooomph and a laugh.

"I want my cuddle time," David claimed, pulling Trace down the hall with him, back to the bedroom. Trace was more than willing. They dropped their clothes on the carpet and climbed onto the huge bed. Trace rolled to his back and stretched luxuriously as David sat next to him and watched. "You're so handsome," David said conversationally.

Trace paused in his stretch and raised an eyebrow. "You know," he said quietly. "I've heard that. A lot, actually. But it means more coming from you."

David smiled and laid down right next to Trace, pulling on his arm. Warmed by a wave of affection swelling in his chest, Trace rolled atop David, sinking them both into the bed. Their bodies aligned from where Trace lay between David's thighs up to their chests, and Trace teased his lips slowly, enjoying being close to David while he cajoled a long, heartfelt kiss from him.

David grinned, enjoying his lover's weight against him. Tilting his head, he sucked at Trace's tongue, his fingers sinking deep into the dark curtain of hair. "Fuck, you taste good."

"Glad you think so," Trace murmured, leisurely kissing his lover again and again.

David basked in the warmth of Trace's body and couldn't overcome the sated lethargy that demanded he just drift for a while. "Hold me while we sleep?"

Trace rolled to his side after one last kiss and curled his arms around David, pulling the other man against him. He tangled their legs together and turned his head so David's tucked into the curve of his neck. "How's that?" he asked softly.

"Perfect."

Trace sighed happily and lifted his hand to caress David's cheek. "We fit," he said simply.

It worked in so many ways, in Trace's opinion. As friends, as companions, as lovers. Drowsy, he started to drift off.

David felt sleep calling, but there was something important he wanted to say. He listened to Trace's soft breathing, wondering if his lover was already asleep. Then he whispered his deepest desire.

"I want you to stay. Stay with me."

He squeezed Trace gently and, reassured, fell asleep.

• Chapter 15

THE soft light of dawn began to brighten the bedroom, waking David. Usually the moment his eyes opened, he was ready for his feet to hit the floor, but waking in Trace's arms, their bodies curled together, legs entwined, he felt no urgency to move. Brushing a lock of dark hair back from Trace's face, he let his fingers linger, tracing the contours. The arch of a cheekbone, a dark brow, the full curve of Trace's bottom lip—every detail was precious.

The whisper-soft touches slowly brought Trace awake, and his eyes fluttered open to see David looking at him tenderly. Trace's pulse picked up. "Morning," he murmured.

"Morning," David returned, his lips curving as they gently touched Trace's. "Sleep well?"

"Mmmm-hmmm," Trace answered, sliding his free hand around David's neck. "Someone tired me out."

David nuzzled Trace's sleep-warm nape. "I feel like I found you just before it was time for you to leave. I don't want to let go."

"So you meant what you said," Trace said slowly.

David realized he must have heard those last words before he fell asleep.

"You want me to stay." He thought it over for a few moments as David remained quiet. "That's an awful big step, isn't it?" he asked seriously.

David closed his eyes, Trace close in his arms, trying not to feel like he was clinging. "I do mean it. Just the idea of going from having you here all the time to not being able to see you every day.... But the last couple of months haven't been normal. It's sort of like falling in love on vacation. I guess we both need to go back to our lives and see where this fits." Pulling away slightly and forcing himself to look Trace in the eye, he said, "But I do want to try this. I want a relationship with you. I don't want to go back to being just friends."

Trace smiled slowly. "Me either. I think I'm going to be lonely in my apartment with just Mabel for company." Trace snorted. "Provided she's willing to go with me. But I think you're right. I want to know this isn't just caused by constant proximity."

"I don't know if constant proximity causes feelings like this, but if it does, I'd be willing to sacrifice and spend all my time with you just to keep it going." David pressed a grin into Trace's shoulder. "Just because you are going home doesn't mean you couldn't keep some stuff here, maybe spend the night occasionally...."

"How about you let me take you to dinner? This weekend?" Trace asked. "Then we can go out somewhere."

"I think I'd rather let you take me to dinner and then stay in." David leered comically. "I should probably warn you. I'm easy."

Trace snorted, grinned, and leaned in to kiss David lightly. "You're on."

"I SHOULD'VE said, 'No, my shoulder aches today, maybe I shouldn't carry anything,'" David complained as they walked out of the elevator and down the hall toward Trace's apartment door.

"Carry?" Trace sent him a tolerant look over his shoulder. "You've got one gym bag—on your good shoulder—and Mabel. I think you'll live." He looked down at the near-overflowing plastic laundry basket he carried.

"Yes, but Mabel's important and not all that happy to be transported," David claimed.

Trace rolled his eyes as he set the basket on the floor next to the door and dug out his keys. "I'm surprised you found her at all, much less got her in the car. I couldn't get her to even come out from under the bed. Wench."

David cleared his throat. "Well…. Catnip *may* have been involved."

Trace snorted as he pushed the door open for the third and final time tonight. "Like I said. Wench. Probably more like her favorite person wanted her to go, and she said 'okay,' I bet." He lifted the basket and led the way inside.

"Mabel likes you," David protested as he pushed the door shut behind them. "Don't you, sweetheart?" he asked as he scratched behind her ears and got loving purrs in return.

"She tolerates me. Because I know where the T-R-E-A-T bag is." Trace set the basket on the floor next to the couch and turned to look at the two, a study in contrast between golden hair and black fur. He shook his head. It was a tossup at this point as to who adored David more, him or Mabel.

"Well, she's back home now, in her own domain, so she should be happy," David said as he set Mabel down on the carpet at his feet. Mabel sniffed and sat down between his ankles.

"That's one of us," Trace murmured as he picked up the garment bag he'd slung over the back of the couch on one of the first trips up from the car. The closer today had gotten, the more unhappy Trace had felt about it. Yeah, he'd agreed that he needed to go back home, so they could make sure this was right and real... "Dammit," Trace cursed under his breath as he headed to the bedroom. "It *is* real."

"What's that?" David called as he started in Trace's direction.

Trace cleared his throat and looked over his shoulder at David. He didn't need to bring it up again; they'd discussed his moving home and why a few times now. "It's going to be a mess getting settled again."

David stopped in the doorway, dropping the gym bag of clothes just inside the threshold. Trace noticed he didn't look all that happy, either. "I'm going to make a pit stop before we take off for dinner," David said, although he lingered.

Trace smiled and nodded. "I'll be ready in a few minutes," he said, nudging the basket with one toe. David smiled, nodded, and disappeared.

Wrinkling his nose, Trace ran one hand through his hair and sat down on the bed. On a whim, he picked up the comforter and held it to his face. Just as quickly, he let it drop. He couldn't catch David's scent on it. Of course he couldn't. He wondered for a minute if David would mind staying over a night or two—

Mabel jumped up out of nowhere, right onto his lap, and swiped at his chin.

"Hey!" Trace protested, leaning back. "What's that for?"

He could have sworn Mabel turned up her nose as she batted at him again before slinking off his lap and onto the comforter, which she proceeded to shred in precise, even slices.

Trace just sighed. "So. Not exactly happy to be home, huh?"

Mabel let out a forlorn little wail, ripped a little more fabric, and then jumped off the bed and disappeared back into the living room.

191

"Yeah," Trace said quietly, watching after her. "I know how you feel."

TRACE shifted in the upholstered waiting room chair. It was right at nine weeks since David's migraine, and Trace thought of the time in blocks: the first couple of weeks being closer friends than ever; almost two weeks of dancing around each other, exploring, testing the waters; a couple more of kissing and touching and cuddling; and since then? More of the same: just longer, hotter, and wetter, and David constantly blowing his mind. Those sorts of memories—like being buried deep in David and coming so hard he could barely breathe—Trace tended to zone out over, disappearing into a cloud of lust-fueled fog.

He startled a little when the door opened. When David walked back out into the waiting room, he stood up and raised an eyebrow, waiting for the news.

"Good as new. No lifting heavy weights for a few more weeks, but I can resume normal activities." David waggled his eyebrows with an exaggerated leer.

Trace blinked and bit his bottom lip on a laugh. He still got caught off guard by David's teasing. He didn't mind so much, other than more than half the time he flushed in response. Some experienced man *he* was. "No heavy weights, huh? Guess that leaves me out then," he answered as they walked out of the building.

"Yeah, guess you'll have to top," David teased, swatting Trace on the ass as he jogged toward the car to stay out of reach.

Eyes widening, Trace choked on a laugh and chased David to the car. Crashing into the side of the convertible and panting with laughter, David turned just as Trace reached him. "You're a funny guy," Trace said, finally catching David against the side panel and gently pushing him against the car, one hand on each side of his waist.

"I'd rather have you think me irresistible," David said, tilting his head and nuzzling Trace's cheek.

Trace sighed and stayed close for a long moment before pulling back. "You have no idea, do you?" he murmured. He was tempted to kiss David right there in the open, where anyone could walk by. *So tempted.* Being this close to David was all it took to arouse him. "Come on. Time to get you home. Got to think about what you'll do now that you have to go back to work every day," he teased.

"You really know how to rain on a guy's good mood," David groused, walking around to the passenger side of the car. "Don't get my kiss *and* I get reminded that I have to go back and put up with the putzes in the newsroom," he muttered as he climbed into the car, fastening his seat belt.

Trace smiled fondly as he got in the driver's seat. He reached over to slide one finger under David's chin, turned it slightly toward him, and pressed a gentle kiss to David's lips. "Does that help?" he asked.

David's eyes closed as he lifted up into the light touch, claiming a real kiss. Lifting his newly released hand to the soft dark hair, he held Trace close, plundering the sweet mouth, sucking at the full lips and swallowing the soft moans escaping from both of them.

Dizzy from just these few kisses, Trace hummed faintly as David took his mouth, freely given. God, Trace wanted to give him so much. He'd be totally calm and under control, and one touch from David would have him flushed and panting. His hand dropped to curl over David's shoulder.

Slowly, even reluctantly, David pulled his mouth away, letting their cheeks press together, Trace's warm moist breath tickling his ear. "*That* helped, but it isn't near enough. How fast can you get us home? I'm in the mood to celebrate my release by doing all sorts of things that involve my right hand and your naked body."

Trace literally whimpered. "I have a meeting at the office in half an hour," he murmured, voice aching.

"Then I guess I'll just have to touch you while you drive," David purred, cupping Trace's erection through his trousers and squeezing.

"Christ," Trace whispered as he started the car with a fierce grin. "Don't let me kill us, okay?"

"You concentrate on driving. I'll concentrate on you," David said, his fingernails scraping up the long inseam of Trace's pants.

Trace gritted his teeth and put the car into reverse, got out of the parking lot and onto the road. He gripped the steering wheel tightly. "Jesus, David, what the fuck are you doing to me?" he asked as he squirmed a little under the other man's hand.

"Oh, come on," David teased with his voice as his hands slipped inside Trace's fly, palming his hot erection. Leaning close to get a better angle, David worked the hard length until the head glistened with beads of fluid. "You can't tell me you've never had someone go down on you in a car."

"Not while I was driving, no!" Trace retorted, lifting his hips a little into David's hand.

"Just don't run off the road, and easy on the gas," David directed as his head dropped into Trace's lap, his tongue finding the edge of the swollen head and tracing the rim.

Trace cried out softly and let off the gas pedal as he drove down the mostly empty city street. He lowered one hand to curl into David's hair. "Oh baby," he whispered, making himself stare at the road. Normally this wouldn't have him so crazy so quickly. But in the car while driving? So dangerous. David's mouth made it amazing.

Aware that they were operating under a timeline, David played dirty. Sucking the shaft into his mouth, he played the ultra-sensitive spot on the underside with his tongue. Pulling Trace even deeper, he hummed and groaned his pleasure, his own hand kneading the bulge in his jeans to release the pressure.

Cursing under his breath, Trace turned onto a busy city street and bit his bottom lip as he forced himself to concentrate. Five blocks, four, three…. "Fuck, David," he hissed as he made the turn onto the quiet street that led into David's subdivision.

David just purred deep in his throat, swallowing around Trace's shaft. Nose buried deep in the musky-smelling curls, he slipped his hand into the loose fabric and cupped the soft sacs, rolling them gently as he lifted his head and sank back down until Trace was sheathed in his throat.

Trace stopped the car in the driveway with a growl, throwing it into park and grabbing David's head with both hands. "David!" he bit out. "Wanna move…." Unwilling to release Trace even long enough to speak, David encouraged him with sound and action. Trace knew David loved making him lose control; he often claimed that, to him, nothing was sexier. Head falling back against the seat, Trace moaned and jutted his hips up, thrusting into David's mouth and throat, feeling it work him all the way down. "Fuck, your gorgeous mouth drives me insane," he breathed, fingers curling in David's hair, panting hard. He was swiftly losing control. "David, David," he moaned, forcing himself to look down at where his cock disappeared into David's mouth. "Oh fuck," he hissed as his groin seized up and he started to tense. "Gonna… gonna…."

David's fingers found the arch of flesh just behind Trace's balls and pressed. Trace's eyes flew open and a yell ripped from him as the sensation crashed through him, throwing him into a wild climax that had him clenching and pulsing into David's mouth. Savoring the taste of Trace on his tongue like a fine wine, David milked the spasming length until it was completely soft, fitting easily inside his mouth. He continued to gently tongue the sated length until Trace had to twitch and wiggle as the stimulation became too much. David let Trace's cock slip from between his lips and rested his head on Trace's thigh.

A shaky hand covered Trace's eyes, the elbow propped against the window, as he tried to pull an even breath. "What the hell did you do to me?" he asked, his voice thick with satiation and a spark of surprise.

"Nothing you don't do to me," David replied, his voice rough with desire.

Trace laughed a bit desperately. "Jesus, you took the top of my head off, lover," he said as he relaxed back into the seat. "We should go in so I can return the favor, but I've got to make this damn meeting."

"I'll hold you to that." David grinned, sitting up and kissing Trace chastely.

Trace ran his tongue along David's lips and growled slightly when he tasted something salty on David's tongue—it had to be his own come. "I can taste myself on you. If that won't make a man hard fast, I don't know what will." He sighed, pulled back, and did up his pants. "I've got to go," he said apologetically.

Trace's reaction to the kiss wound David up more than the blow job had. Straightening in his seat, he reached for the door. "I'll see you tonight," he said, pulling on the lever and unfolding his body from the low sports car. Adjusting himself with the heel of his hand, he silently gave thanks that his arm was healed. It was about to get a workout.

WITH a happy sigh, Trace rolled out of bed and stretched. He'd gotten home after the meeting and dragged David into their bedroom, fully intent on celebrating David's new freedom. And David had been very appreciative as Trace sucked him until he came, screaming, and then moaned as Trace jacked off against him, splattering them both with his come.

Trace figured he never would have thought that life with David would be so incredibly sensual. He smiled as he climbed back into his shorts and T-shirt, and then he pulled out some clothes for David as well. Having him unclothed within reach would be distracting as hell.

"I brought you these, you exhibitionist," Trace teased as he entered the kitchen to find David putting a piece of very rich cheesecake on a plate.

"You love my exhibitionist ass," David said with a wink as he put the rest of the cake back in the fridge. "Besides, I was bringing this back to bed. We're celebrating, after all."

"Celebrating being done with early mornings, thank God," Trace agreed.

"I thought you liked early mornings with me," David allowed as he grabbed one fork and the plate and started back down the hall.

Trace's eyes followed David's ass every step of the way. "Yeah, sure," he said distractedly.

David chuckled and climbed onto the bed. "C'mon, handsome. Have some cheesecake."

"This is ridiculously romantic, you know," Trace said, waving his hand around at the flickering candles, the cheesecake, and the very high-grade Egyptian cotton sheets. That he'd bought himself.

David slid a bite between his lips, and Trace's eyes grew larger as he watched David's tongue stroke over the tines of the fork. Clearing his throat, he rubbed himself through his sweats before stripping them off and joining David on the sheets, sitting cross-legged next to him.

"Open sesame," David drawled, holding out a deliciously decadent bite of double dark chocolate fudge cheesecake.

Trace felt it start melting as soon as it hit his tongue, and he groaned pitifully. "One bite and you cannot imagine the sugar rush."

"Oh, I can imagine," David corrected. Trace reached out and took the fork, feeding David a bite. David made obscenely wonderful sounds of appreciation, and Trace's cock reacted, drawing a smile from them both. "Already?" David teased as they shared bites. "I would have thought I'd worn you out."

Trace worked on suckling the chocolate from the fork as he turned his idea over in his mind for what had to be the thousandth time. "No, I'm good," he demurred. "Now that your shoulder's all healed up, you're going to need your strength."

"Is that so?" David asked. Trace could see the candlelight flickering in his blue eyes.

"Yeah," Trace bypassed the fork and went for David's lips. After a long, drawn-out kiss, he murmured against David's lips. "I want you to make love to me."

"I always make love to you."

True. But this time Trace wanted so much more. He reached down slowly to trail his fingers over David's half-hard cock. "I want you to make love to me," he repeated. "I want you in me. I want to feel you, feel you come inside me, feel it wet and slick between my thighs afterward. Knowing it's all you."

David shivered bodily as he stared. He opened his mouth to speak, but nothing came out of his trembling lips.

"It's okay," Trace soothed, kissing him again. "I trust you."

"Oh baby," David said brokenly, his hands moving to cup Trace's face. "I love you so much."

"I know," Trace said, turning his head so he could kiss David's palm. "I love you too."

• Epilogue

"C'MON David, don't make me get up there," Trace wheedled, turning sideways in the chair at the decorated table. "You know what Katherine's like." Around the table, Matt snorted.

"This isn't about Katherine, lover. This is about the kids over at St. Vincent's." David ran his hand up Trace's thigh under the table, squeezing. "Besides, I want to see your ass walk across that stage and know that it's all mine," he added in a hoarse whisper, close to Trace's ear.

Trace closed his eyes for a few seconds before looking at the other man. He rolled his eyes, although the gesture was affectionate. "You better not lose," he warned, pushing out of the chair as the host called his name a second time and the audience cheered. It was the annual fund-raiser for the children's hospital, an event of glitz and glamour, and all the biggest names in town showed up.

"I can't believe you're actually throwing him to the wolves," Matt said, raising his scotch to his lips.

David grinned, watching the hands fly up all over the room as the bidding started after the host introduced Trace. "It won't hurt him to sweat a little. Then I can swoop in and save him like a knight in shining armor."

"I think you're mixing your metaphors. Superheroes swoop. Knights ride."

David glared at his friend, kicking at him under the table. "You know what I mean."

Ever the social butterfly, Trace hammed it up on stage, encouraging the bids. The last several years he'd brought in one of the top five or so offers, and judging by the furious bidding going on now, it looked like it would happen again. A few of the women even approached the stage to ask questions, and Trace squatted down to talk to them, smiling all the while.

David tilted his head, appreciating the stretch of fabric over Trace's ass as he talked to a pretty brunette. The first few months of their relationship, he'd constantly tormented himself with the thought of Trace announcing that the experiment was over and he really preferred women, but all those doubts had systematically been extinguished by the steady deepening of their relationship. David had never loved this way before, and he knew now that love was returned absolutely.

"She's making her move." David's shoulders tensed as Matt nudged him. The photographer nodded at the elegant blonde columnist maneuvering forward through the crowd.

There was a gaggle of women at the edge of the stage now, alternately talking and bidding as Trace flirted outrageously, driving up the bid. In the middle of it all, Trace glanced over and made eye contact with David, deliberately winking. Several of the women sighed and mock-swooned, drawing a warm laugh from the journalist on stage.

"God, he's a terrible flirt. How do you stand it?" asked Patrick, who was sitting next to Matt. "I think he's worse than me!"

"Because I know where he spends his nights. *All* his nights," David answered, smiling fondly. His friends around the table laughed, knowing that full well.

Trace stood up and looked over the group, and out of nowhere the bid jumped significantly, gaining a lot of hostile stares from the other women. Katherine glided through to the front of the stage. "You're not escaping me this time, Jackson," she promised.

Trace slid a hand into his pocket and, calculatingly, just barely slid his tongue over his bottom lip. "We'll see about that, darlin'," Trace teased. The rest of the group started whispering and looking at them both, and two more women made bids.

Katherine looked at the host. "I bid one thousand dollars."

Trace blinked in surprise and couldn't stifle a small laugh.

"This is going to cost you a fortune," Matt said, looking at Trace's casually seductive pose.

"It's worth every penny," David said quietly before raising his voice. "Twelve hundred."

Katherine sent a scathing glare over her shoulder toward their table, thinking they were just messing with her again. "Two thousand!" She smirked, believing that would shut them up.

"Twenty-five hundred," David came back.

Katherine narrowed her eyes and looked back at Trace accusingly. It was obvious he was really amused, eyes bright. He gave her a small smile and shrugged casually with one shoulder.

The blonde crossed her arms, starting to look more annoyed than usual. "Three thousand," she said petulantly, drawing copious applause and hooting from the crowd. It was the highest bid seen in several years.

"You could just let her win," Matt suggested. "It's not like he'd actually sleep with her or anything."

David shuddered. "I wouldn't be sleeping with him either, if I pulled a stunt like that, and, as you know, my couch isn't that comfortable." Standing, he mirrored Trace's casual pose and leaned back against a draped column. "Five thousand dollars."

The room erupted in gasps and catcalls, and all eyes turned on Katherine, who was really red in the face. She shot Trace a look promising torture and death, and he just chuckled, drawing more laughter.

"Five thousand dollars, going once," the host said. After a moment she added, "Going twice," and looked intently at Katherine, who stamped her foot and turned away, stalking back to her table. A lot of the other women grinned and looked back at David, then up to Trace, who was on stage with a silly grin on his face. "Sold!"

David strolled up to the stage, extending his hand and helping Trace down. When Trace reached the floor, he threaded their fingers together and held on. Amid loud applause and raucous laughter and yelling, Trace grinned lovingly, pulled up close to David, and kissed him sweetly right then and there.

David's lips curved into a smile under Trace's. "You are going to catch no end of shit for this, you know?" he whispered to his lover, squeezing his hand.

Trace tossed his head back and laughed, carefree, as the squeals and hooting echoed through the room. "Hope so," he said. "You deserve a kiss after spending that amount of money on me."

"I'd better get more than that," David pouted. "Let's go home, lover."

As they passed Katherine, the columnist's normally pristine look ruined by her incredulous gape, David leaned toward her. "Can't have you getting a chance to grope my boyfriend." Then he and Trace walked on.

"What...? How...? When did that happen?" Katherine spluttered as Matt strolled up to her side, grinning at the silhouette of his departing friends, shoulder to shoulder, hand in hand.

"Months ago, but they moved in together last weekend. I think you can cross Trace off your list as the one that got away."

RHIANNE AILE has an unhealthy relationship with her computer, iced tea, and chocolate. Growing up, she split her time between Oklahoma and Chicago, making her equally fond of horses, skyscrapers, cowboys, and men in well-tailored suits. Facilitating retreats for women and authors keeps her traveling enough to stay happy.

Visit her Web site at http://www.rhianneaile.com/ and her blog at http://rhianne-aile.livejournal.com/.

MADELEINE URBAN is a down-home Kentucky girl who's been writing since she could hold a crayon. Although she has written and published on her own, she truly excels when writing with co-authors. She lives with her husband, who is very supportive of her work, and two canine kids who only allow her to hug them when she has food. She wants to live at Disney World, the home of fairy dust, because she believes that with hard work, a little luck, and beloved family and friends, dreams really can come true.

Visit Madeleine's blog at http://www.madeleineurban.com or http://madeleineurban.livejournal.com/. You can contact her at mrs.madeleine.urban@gmail.com.

Other titles by RHIANNE AILE

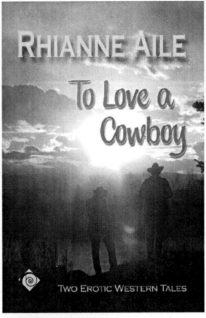

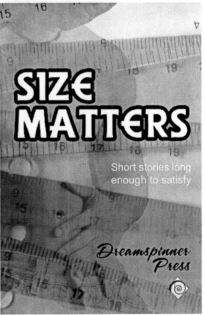

http://www.dreamspinnerpress.com

Other titles by MADELEINE URBAN

LaVergne, TN USA
28 December 2009

168191LV00005B/32/P